环环词汇轻松记

挑战 新概念英语1

核心词汇

王月 等◎编

U0117100

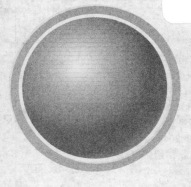

中国水利水电出版社
www.waterpub.com.cn

内 容 提 要

本书以词汇记忆大连串为主线，通过大家熟悉的练习形式，帮助读者在不经意间构建出属于自己的词库，提高英语水平。

本书适用于学习《新概念英语》（第一册）的读者。

图书在版编目（CIP）数据

挑战新概念英语核心词汇. 第 1 册 / 王月等编. —北京：中国水利水电出版社，2009
（环环词汇轻松记）
ISBN 978 - 7 - 5084 - 6000 - 0

Ⅰ. 挑… Ⅱ. 王… Ⅲ. 英语—词汇—自学参考资料 Ⅳ. H313

中国版本图书馆 CIP 数据核字（2008）第 166477 号

书　　名	环环词汇轻松记 **挑战新概念英语 1 核心词汇**	
作　　者	王月 等 编	
出版发行	中国水利水电出版社（北京市三里河路 6 号　100044） 网址：www.waterpub.com.cn E-mail：sales@waterpub.com.cn 电话：(010) 63202266（总机）、68367658（营销中心）	
经　　售	北京科水图书销售中心（零售） 电话：(010) 88383994、63202643 全国各地新华书店和相关出版物销售网点	
排　　版	贵艺图文设计中心	
印　　刷	北京市地矿印刷厂	
规　　格	145mm×210mm　32 开本　13.25 印张　437 千字	
版　　次	2009 年 1 月第 1 版　2009 年 1 月第 1 次印刷	
印　　数	0001—5000 册	
定　　价	**24.80 元**	

挑战新概念英语 1
核心词汇

主　编　王　月

编　委　王　月　　段其刚　　彭乃鹏　　丁　静
　　　　庞天翔　　黄　毅　　刘翠楠　　曹　畅
　　　　郭丽萍　　王福强　　王文敏　　郑崑琳
　　　　韩利俊　　陈轶斐　　郑　炎　　郭　丹静
　　　　郭宗炎　　侯卫群　　刘　洋　　艾　静

Contents

目 录

Lesson 1

Excuse me!

对不起！

I New words 新单词

1. **excuse** *v.* 原谅

> excuse *v.* 原谅
> excuse *n.* 饶恕，借口
> excusal *n.* 原谅，免除（税款或罚款等）
> excusable *adj.* 可原谅的

_____ his bad manners.

2. **me** *pron.* 我（宾格）

> me *pron.* 我（宾格）
> I *pron.* 我（主格）
> My *pron.* 我的

This letter is addressed to _____ .

3. **yes** *adv.* 是的

> yes *adv.* 是的
> yes *n.* 赞成票
> no *adv.* 不，毫不

Do you want that? _____ , I do.

4. **is** *v.* be 动词现在时第三人称单数

> is   *v.* be 动词现在时第三人称单数
>
> am   *v.* be 动词现在时第一人称单数
>
> are   *v.* be 动词现在时第二人称单数

She _____ Peter's sister.

5. **this**   *pron.* 这

> this   *pron.* 这
>
> that   *pron.* 那
>
> these   *pron.* 这些
>
> those   *pron.* 那些

_____ is my coat.

6. **your**   *pron. & adj.* 你的；你们的

> your   *pron. & adj.* 你的；你们的
>
> you   *pron.* 你，你们

The light switch is on _____ right.

7. **handbag**   *n.*（女用）手提包

> handbag   *n.*（女用）手提包
>
> handbag tag   *n.* 行李牌
>
> handball   *n.* 手球
>
> handbell   *n.* 手铃

She reached into her _____ and found a comb.

8. **pardon**   *int.* 原谅，请再说一遍

> pardon   *int.* 原谅，请再说一遍
>
> beg your pardon   对不起，请原谅
>
> pardonable   *adj.* 可原谅的
>
> pardoner   *n.* 宽恕的人

I beg your _____?

9. **it** *pron.* 它

> it　*pron.* 它
> it's it is 或 it has 的缩写

This is my watch , _____ is a Swiss one.

10. **thank you** 感谢你（们）

> thank you　感谢你（们）
> thankful　*adj.* 感谢的，感激的
> thankfully　*adv.* 感谢地，感激地
> thankfulness　*n.* 感谢，感激

No , _____ , I don't want any more tea.

11. **very much** 非常地

> very much　非常地
> very good　很好
> very deed　实际上，真的

She was _____ interested.

II Make sentences using the under-mentioned words 单词造句

excuse — me

_____ .

your — pardon

_____ .

this — handbag

_____ .

yes — thank you

_____ .

it — very much

_____ .

is — your

_____.

III Match 连线

- to forgive（someone）for a small fault used esp. as   your
- objective form of I   very much
- used as an answer expressing agreement or willingness   it
- third person sing，present tense of BE   thank you
- being the person，thing，idea，etc.，which is understood or（about to be）mentioned   me
- of or belonging to you   excuse
- a small bag，esp. one used by a woman to carry her money and personal things in   is
- to forgive or excuse   pardon
- that thing，group，idea，etc.，already mentioned   yes
- used politely to mean I am grateful to you   handbag
- （used for giving force to an expression）especially to a great degree   this

IV Glossary 词汇表

excuse *v.* 原谅
me *pron.* 我（宾格）
yes *adv.* 是的
is *v.* be 动词现在时第三人称单数
this *pron.* 这
your *pron. & adj.* 你的；你们的
handbag *n.* （女用）手提包

pardon   *int.* 原谅，请再说一遍
it   *pron.* 它
thank you   感谢你（们）
very much   非常地

Lesson 2

Is this your...?
这是你的……吗?

1. **pen** *n.* 钢笔

> pen *n.* 钢笔
> pen *v.* 写
> pen friend *n.* 笔友
> pen name *n.* 笔名

Today is my birthday, so my mother bought a _____ as my birthday present.

2. **pencil** *n.* 铅笔

> pencil *n.* 铅笔
> pencil *v.* 暂时接纳，暂记下
> ballpoint pen *n.* 圆珠笔
> fountain pen *n.* 自来水钢笔
> pencil case *n.* 铅笔盒
> pencil sharpener *n.* 铅笔刀

He is sharpening his _____ with a pencil sharpener.

3. **book** *n.* 书

> book *n.* 书，书籍
> book *v.* 登记，预告

> book bank　*n.* 旧书店
> book cabinet　*n.* 书柜

She is writing a _____ about her traveling in England.

4. **watch**　*n.* 手表

> watch　*n.* 手表
> watch　*v.* 观看，注视，注意
> watch band　*n.* 手表带
> watch case　*n.* 表壳

This _____ doesn't work.

5. **coat**　*n.* 上衣，外衣

> coat　*n.* 上衣，外衣
> coat　*v.* 涂上，包上
> coat-hanger　*n.* 衣架
> coat of arms　*n.* 盾形纹章，盾徽

Your _____ is very dirty.

6. **dress**　*n.* 连衣裙

> dress　*n.* 连衣裙
> dress　*v.* 穿衣服
> dress coat　*n.* 燕尾服
> dress smock　*n.* 披风

The mother bought a very beautiful _____ for her little daughter.

7. **skirt**　*n.* 裙子

> skirt　*n.* 裙子
> T-skirt　*n.* 衬衫
> dress　*n.* 连衣裙
> coat　*n.* 风衣，大衣
> sweater　*n.* 运动衫

The _____ looks beautiful.

8. **shirt**   *n.* 衬衣

> shirt   *n.* 衬衣
> shirt-sleeve   *n.* 衬衫袖子；*adj.* 爽直的
> shirtband   *n.* 衬衫的襟子
> shirted   *n.* 穿着衬衫的人

This _____ is very expensive.

9. **car**   *n.* 小汽车

> car   *n.* 小汽车
> boat   *n.* 船
> bus   *n.* 公共汽车
> plane   *n.* 飞机

My _____ is over there.

10. **house**   *n.* 房子

> house   *n.* 房子
> house   *v.* 给……房子住，收藏，躲藏
> flat   *n.* 公寓
> home   *n.* 家

Do you live in a _____ or a flat?

Ⅱ *Make sentences using the under-mentioned words* 单词造句

pen — book

_____.

car — house

_____.

time — watch

_____.

coat — shirt

_____.

dress — party

_____.

pencil — pencil sharpener

_____.

Ⅲ Match 连线

- an instrument for writing or drawing with ink
- a narrow pointed usu. wooden instrument used for writing or drawing, containing a thin stick of a black or colored material
- a number of printed or written sheets of paper bound together in a cover
- a small clock to be worn, esp. on the wrist, or carried
- long outer garment with sleeves, usu. fastened at the front with buttons
- an outer garment for a woman or girl, with or without sleeves, that covers the body from shoulder to knee or below
- a piece of clothing for the upper part of the body that is usu. of light cloth with a collar and sleeves, is fastened in front with buttons, and is typically worn by a man
- a road vehicle with usu. four wheels which is driven by a motor and used as a manes of travel for a small number of people
- a building for people to live in, usu. one that has more than one level and is intended for use by a single family

watch

book

car

pen

pencil

shirt

house

dress

coat

IV Glossary 词汇表

pen   *n.* 钢笔

pencil   *n.* 铅笔

book   *n.* 书

watch   *n.* 手表

coat   *n.* 上衣，外衣

dress   *n.* 连衣裙

skirt   *n.* 裙子

shirt   *n.* 衬衣

car   *n.* 小汽车

house   *n.* 房子

Lesson 3

Sorry, sir.

对不起, 先生。

New words 新单词 ·

1. **umbrella** *n.* 伞

   > umbrella *n.* 伞
   > parachute *n.* 降落伞
   > umbrellalike *adj.* 伞状的

   Take an _____ — it's going to rain.

2. **please** *int.* 请

   > please *int.* 请
   > please *adj.* 满足的; *v.* 请, 使喜欢, 取悦
   > if you please 劳驾

   May I help you? _____.

3. **here** *adv.* 这里

   > here *adv.* 这里
   > there *adv.* 那里
   > where *adv.* 在哪里

   Stop _____ for a rest.

4. **my** *pron. & adj.* 我的

   > my *pron. & adj.* 我的
   > your *pron. & adj.* 你的

> her　*pron. & adj.* 她的
> his　*pron. & adj.* 他的
> their　*pron. & adj.* 他们的

This is _____ rooter.

5. **ticket**　*n.* 票

> ticket　*n.* 票
> ticket-collector　*n.* 检票员
> ticket agency　*n.* 售票代理处
> ticket agent　*n.* 售票代理人

We buy a _____ to get a seat on a bus, train, or airplane.

6. **number**　*n.* 号码

> number　*n.* 号码
> number one　*n.* 第一，最好
> number two　*n.* 第二流的

We live at _____ 102 Church Street.

7. **five**　*num.* 五

> five　*num.* 五
> five-star　*adj.* 第一流的，五星级的
> five-day week　*n.* 每周五天工作日
> five-year plan　（经济建设）五年计划

It is a _____ -star hotel you ordered yesterday.

8. **sorry**　*adj.* 对不起的

> sorry　*adj.* 对不起的
> excuse me　　对不起

I was _____ to hear about your illness.

9. **sir**   *n.* 先生

> sir   *n.* 先生
> gentleman   *n.* 先生
> lady   *n.* 女士
> madam   *n.* 女士，夫人

Come here at once, _____ !

10. **cloakroom**   *n.* 衣帽存放处

> cloakroom   *n.* 衣帽存放处
> cloak room ticket   寄存票
> clothes tree   衣帽架

Please leave the coat in the _____.

II Make sentences using the under-mentioned words 单词造句

umbrella — here

_____ .

please — ticket

_____ .

my — number

_____ .

sorry — sir

_____ .

five — cloakroom

_____ .

III Match 连线

- an arrangement of cloth over a folding frame with   my
  a handle, used for keeping rain off the head

- used when asking politely for something   please
- at, in, or to this place or point   umbrella
- of or belonging to me   ticket
- written or printed piece of paper or card given to   sorry
  someone to show that they have paid for a service
  such as a journey on a bus, entrance into a
  cinema, etc.
- a number used to show the position of something   five
  in an ordered set or list
- the cardinal number 5   sir
- feeling pity or sympathy, wretched   cloakroom
- respectful form of address to a man; title of a   here
  knight
- a room, e.g. in a theatre, where hats, coats,   number
  etc., maybe left for a short time

Ⅳ Glossary 词汇表

umbrella   *n.* 伞

please   *int.* 请

here   *adv.* 这里

my   *pron. & adj.* 我的

ticket   *n.* 票

number   *n.* 号码

five   *num.* 五

sorry   *adj.* 对不起的

sir   *n.* 先生

cloakroom   *n.* 衣帽存放处

4

Is this your...?

这是你的……吗？

I New words 新单词

1. **suit**   *n.* 一套衣服

   > suit   *n.* 一套衣服
   > swimsuit   *n.* 游泳衣
   > spacesuit   *n.* 太空服，航天服

   The _____ suits you very well.

2. **school**   *n.* 学校

   > school   *n.* 学校
   > college   *n.* 学院
   > university   *n.* 大学
   > seminary   *n.* 神学院

   He is old enough for _____.

3. **teacher**   *n.* 老师

   > teacher   *n.* 老师
   > tutor   *n.* 家庭教师，大学指导教师，助教
   > teacher's day   教师节
   > student   *n.* 学生

   My mother is a _____ of a middleschool.

4. **son**   *n.* 儿子

> son   *n.* 儿子
> boy   *n.* 男孩
> son-in-law   *n.* 女婿，养子
> son and heir   子嗣

His _____ is not at home now.

5. **daughter**   *n.* 女儿

> daughter   *n.* 女儿
> girl   *n.* 女孩
> daughter-in-law   *n.* 儿媳妇

They have a lovely _____ .

II Make sentences using the under-mentioned words 单词造句

suit — teacher

_____.

son — school

_____.

daughter — beautiful

_____.

III Match 连线

- set of clothes   daughter
- institution for education   son
- person who teaches and is usually employed by a   suit
  school
- male offspring; male descendent   school
- one's male child   teacher

IV Glossary 词汇表

suit   *n.* 一套衣服
school   *n.* 学校
teacher   *n.* 老师
son   *n.* 儿子
daughter   *n.* 女儿

Nice to meet you!
很高兴见到你!

I New words 新单词

1. **Mr**. *n*. 先生

> Mr.　*n*. 先生
> gentleman　*n*. 先生，有身份的人
> sir　*n*. 先生

_____ Wang teaches us maths.

2. **good** *adj*. 好

> good　*adj*. 好
> fine　*adj*. 美好的，优良的
> kind　*adj*. 亲切的，和蔼的
> nice　*adj*. 美好的，精密的，好的

The opera had a _____ press.

3. **morning** *n*. 早晨

> morning　*n*. 早晨
> afternoon　*n*. 下午
> evening　*n*. 傍晚

This _____, I went to school.

4. **Miss** *n*. 小姐

> Miss　小姐
> lady　*n*. 女士，夫人

Mrs.　*n.* 夫人

woman　*n.* 女人，妇女

_____ Liu is a taxi driver.

5. **new**　*adj.* 新的

new　*adj.* 新的

newly　*adv.* 重新，最近的，以新的方式

fresh　*adj.* 新鲜的，无经验的

old　*adj.* 旧的

She is learning a _____ language.

6. **student**　*n.* 学生

student　*n.* 学生

pupil　*n.* 学生，小学生

scholastic　*n.* 学生，学究

student union　学生会

He is a _____ of history.

7. **French**　*adj. & n.* 法国的；法国人

French　*adj. & n.* 法国的；法国人

Frenchman　*n.* 法国人

Frenchwoman　*n.* 法国女人

French window　*n.* 落地窗

France　*n.* 法国，法兰西

His major is _____.

8. **German**　*adj. & n.* 德国的；德国人

German　*adj. & n.* 德国的；德国人

German black　德国黑

> German orange　德国橙
> Germany　*n.* 德国

Do you have any friend of _____?

9. **nice** *adj.* 美好的

> nice　*adj.* 美好的
> nicely　*adv.* 精细地
> nice-looking　*adj.* 好看的

We have a _____ trip to France.

10. **meet** *v.* 遇见

> meet　*v.* 遇见
> meet by chance　偶然遇见
> encounter　*v.* 遭遇，遇见
> see　*v.* 看见

I _____ her in the street just now.

11. **Japanese** *adj. & n.* 日本的；日本人

> Japanese　*adj. & n.* 日本的；日本人
> Japan　*n.* 日本
> Japannish　日本式的

Can you speak _____?

12. **Korean** *adj. & n.* 韩国的；韩国人

> Korean　*adj. & n.* 韩国的；韩国人
> Korea　*n.* 韩国

We have a teacher of _____.

13. **Chinese** *adj. & n.* 中国的；中国人

> Chinese　*adj. & n.* 中国的；中国人
> China　*n.* 中国

Many foreigners are very interested in _____ traditional culture.

14. **too**   *adv.* 也

> too   *adv.* 也
>
> also   *adv.* 也，同样
>
> either   *conj.* 也，或者；*adj.* 两者任一的

I like bananas, but I like oranges, _____.

II Make sentences using the under-mentioned words 单词造句

Mr. — Japanese

_____.

good — Korean

_____.

Miss — French

_____.

new — student

_____.

German — meet

_____.

nice — Chinese

_____.

Good — too

_____.

III Match 连线

- title prefixed to a man's name
- morally correct or kind; having positive or desirable qualities Chinese title of a girl or unmarried woman
- something not existing before, and has now been discovered, made or experienced

meet

Korean

too

- a person engaged in studying something, especially at a college or university   nice
- the standard language of France and other French speaking countries   Japanese
- the language spoken by Germans   German
- pleasing or friendly   French
- come together and see others again   student
- of Japan or the language spoken by the people of japan   new
- of Korea or the language spoken by the people of korea   Miss
- a person who is born in or lives in China; the language spoken in China   good
- to a greater extent than is desirable; very; also   Mr.

Ⅳ Glossary 词汇表

Mr. *n.* 先生
good *adj.* 好
morning *n.* 早晨
Miss *n.* 小姐
new *adj.* 新的
student *n.* 学生
French *adj. & n.* 法国的；法国人
German *adj. & n.* 德国的；德国人
nice *adj.* 美好的
meet *v.* 遇见
Japanese *adj. & n.* 日本的；日本人
Korean *adj. & n.* 韩国的；韩国人
Chinese *adj. & n.* 中国的；中国人
too *adv.* 也

Lesson 6

What make is it?
它是什么牌子的？

I New words 新单词

1. **make** *n.* （产品的）牌号

> make *n.* （产品的）牌号
> make *v.* 做，制造
> trademark *n.* 商标
> brand *n.* 商标，牌子，烙印

This is a famous _____ of shirt.

2. **Swedish** *adj.* 瑞典的

> Swedish *adj.* 瑞典的
> Sweden *n.* 瑞典
> Swede *n.* 瑞典人

She can sing several _____ songs.

3. **English** *adj.* 英国的

> English *adj.* 英国的
> England *n.* 英格兰（英国的主要部分）
> Englander *n.* 英格兰人，英国人
> British *adj.* 大不列颠的，英国的，英国人的

He can speak _____ fluently.

4. **American** *adj.* 美国的

> American   *adj.* 美国的
> America   *n.* 美国，美洲（包括北美和南美）
> United states   美国
> U. S. A.   美国

One of the most basic moral values for _____ is honesty.

5. **Italian**   *adj.* 意大利的

> Italian   *adj.* 意大利的
> Italia   *n.* 意大利
> Italy   *n.* 意大利

Do you like _____ food?

6. **Volvo**   *n.* 沃尔沃

Do you like _____?

7. **Peugeot**   *n.* 标致

_____ is my favorite brand.

8. **Mercedes**   *n.* 梅赛德斯

> Mercedes   *n.* 梅赛德斯
> Mercedes   *n.* 莫西迪斯（女名）
> Mercedes-Benz   奔驰汽车

_____ is a world famous brand.

9. **Toyota**   *n.* 丰田

> Toyota   *n.* 丰田
> Tokyo   *n.* 东京（日本首都）

_____ comes from Japan.

10. **Daewoo**   *n.* 大宇

He bought a _____ last year.

11. **Mini** *n.* 迷你

> Mini　*n.* 迷你
>
> Mini skirt　*n.* 迷你裙，超短裙
>
> Mini bus　*n.* 小型公共汽车，小巴士

Many ladies like _____ very much.

12. **Ford** *n.* 福特

> Ford　*n.* 福特
>
> Ford　*n.* 福特汽车公司，姓氏

He drives his _____ to work every day.

13. **Fiat** *n.* 菲亚特

> Fiat　*n.* 菲亚特
>
> Fiat　*n.* 菲亚特汽车公司

The headquarters of _____ Group is in Italy.

Ⅱ Make sentences using the under-mentioned words 单词造句

make — Toyota

_____

Italian — Fiat

_____

English — Mini

_____

American — Ford

_____

Daewoo — Korean

_____

Mercedes — German

_____

Peugeot — French

_____.

Volvo — Swedish

_____.

Ⅲ Match 连线

- a type of product, esp. as produced by a particular maker

  Fiat

- of Sweden or the language spoken by the people of sweden

  Mini

- of England or the language spoken by the people of England

  Ford

- of American or the language spoken by the people of American

  Daewoo

- of Italian or the language spoken by the people of Italian

  Toyota

- a kind of car made inSweden

  Mercedes

- a kind of car made in French

  Peugeot

- a kind of car made in German

  Volvo

- a kind of car made in Japan

  Italian

- a kind of car made in Korea

  American

- a kind of clothes made in England

  English

- a kind of car made in American

  Swedish

- a kind of car made in Italy

  make

Ⅳ Glossary 词汇表

make *n.* （产品的）牌号

Swedish *adj.* 瑞典的

English   *adj.* 英国的

American   *adj.* 美国的

Italian   *adj.* 意大利的

Volvo   *n.* 沃尔沃

Peugeot   *n.* 标致

Mercedes   *n.* 梅赛德斯

Toyota   *n.* 丰田

Daewoo   *n.* 大宇

Mini   *n.* 迷你

Ford   *n.* 福特

Fiat   *n.* 菲亚特

Are you a teacher?
你是教师吗?

I New words 新单词 ....

1. **I** *pron.* 我

> I *pron.* 我（主格）
> me *pron.* 我（宾格）

Mum, _____ see an airplane in the sky.

2. **am** *v.* be 动词现在时第一人称单数

> am *v.* be 动词现在时第一人称单数
> is *v.* be 动词现在时第三人称单数

I _____ waiting for you at the school gate.

3. **are** *v.* be 动词现在时复数

> are *v.* be 动词现在时复数
> were *v.* be 动词过去时复数

You _____ my friend.

4. **name** *n.* 名字

> name *n.* 名字; *v.* 命名
> moniker *n.* 名字, 绰号

May I ask your _____?

5. **what** *adj. & pron.* 什么

what	adj. & pron.	什么
where	adv.	什么地方
which	adj. & pron.	哪个

_____ is on the desk?

6. **nationality** n. 国籍

nationality	n.	国籍
national	adj.	国家的，民族的
nationally	adv.	全国性，举国一致

Richard is American, John is British — they have different _____.

7. **job** n. 工作

job	n.	工作
work	n.	工作，职业，作品; v. 工作，经营
job-hunt	v.	找工作
position	n.	职位，位置

My mother does all the _____ about the house.

8. **keyboard** n. 电脑键盘

keyboard	n.	电脑键盘
keyboard entry	n.	键盘输入
keyboard input		键入
keyboard speed	n.	键盘速度

You should never eat by your computer _____ or it might get dirty.

9. **operator** n. 操作人员

operator	n.	操作人员
operator error		操作者误差
operate	v.	操作，运转

Ask the _____ to put you through.

10. **engineer** *n.* 工程师

> engineer *n.* 工程师
> engineer in chief 总工程师
> engineering *n.* 工程学

Mike's an electrical _____.

II Make sentences using the under-mentioned words 单词造句

I — am

_____.

are — nationality

_____.

name — what

_____.

job — engineer

_____.

keyboard — operator

_____.

III Match 连线

- person who is the speaker or writer and is referring to himself or herself
- 1st person sing. Present tense of BE
- present tense indicative plural and second person singular of BE
- title of a person, thing, etc.
- asking for the name, reason, etc. of something

engineer

operator

keyboard

job

nationality

- status of belonging to a specific country   what
- piece of work; task; a duty or responsbility   name
- a row or several rows of keys on musical   are
  instrument or a machine
- person who operates   am
- person skilled in engineering   I

IV Glossary 词汇表

I   *pron.* 我

am   *v.* be 动词现在时第一人称单数

are   *v.* be 动词现在时复数

name   *n.* 名字

what   *adj. & pron.* 什么

nationality   *n.* 国籍

job   *n.* 工作

keyboard   *n.* 电脑键盘

operator   *n.* 操作人员

engineer   *n.* 工程师

8

What's your job?
你是做什么工作的？

I New words 新单词

1. **policeman** *n.* 警察

> policeman *n.* 警察
> police office 警察局
> police officer 警官

Don't you think that the _____ might be the best people to ask for help?

2. **policewoman** *n.* 女警察

> policewoman *n.* 女警察
> police matron 女看守，女管理员
> police dog 警犬

Have you ever seen the film "Chinese _____"?

3. **taxi driver** 出租汽车司机

> taxi driver 出租汽车司机
> taxi *n.* 出租汽车；*v.* 乘坐出租汽车
> taxi-rank *n.* 出租汽车停车处
> taxi meter 计程器

Most of the _____ work overtime every day.

4. **air hostess** 空中小姐

air hostess 空中小姐

airman *n.* 飞行员，空军

pilot *n.* 飞行员，领航员

trainman *n.* 乘务员，（铁路）车务员

steward *n.*（轮船、飞机等）乘务员

_____ is an enviable job.

5. **postman** *n.* 邮递员

postman *n.* 邮递员

postage *n.* 邮费

post *n.* 邮件

The _____ delivered a mail to her.

6. **nurse** *n.* 护士

nurse *n.* 护士

charge nurse 护士长

doctor *n.* 医生

patient *n.* 病人

She works as a _____ in a hospital.

7. **mechanic** *n.* 机械师

mechanic *n.* 机械师

mechanical *adj.* 机械的，机械制的，机械似的，呆板的

engineman *n.* 操纵引擎者，（工厂等中的）机械师

machinist *n.* 机械师，机械工，机械安装修

The _____ is repairing the equipment.

8. **hairdresser** *n.* 理发师

hairdresser　*n.* 理发师
hairdress　*n.* ＜美＞（好）发型，发式
hairdressing　*n.* 理发，美发，美容
barber　*n.* 理发员，理发师；*v.* 为……理发，刮脸等

A _____ is someone whose occupation is to cut or style hair.

9. **housewife**　*n.* 家庭妇女

housewife　*n.* 家庭妇女
housewifely　*adj.* 主妇们的，节俭的
housework　*n.* 家务，劳动，家务事
career woman　*n.* 职业妇女

Do you want to be a _____?

10. **milkman**　*n.* 送牛奶的人

milkman　*n.* 送牛奶的人
milk-float　*n.* 送牛奶马车
milkmaid　*n.* 挤奶的妇女，在奶酪农场工作
milkness　*n.* 牛奶的产量

The _____ gets up to work very early every day.

Ⅱ *Make sentences using the under-mentioned words* 单词造句

policeman — policewoman

_____.

taxi driver — nurse

_____.

air hostess — hairdresser

_____.

postman — housewife

_____.

mechanic — milkman

_____.

Ⅲ Match 连线

- male member of police force
- female member of police force
- person who drives a taxi
- a woman who looks after the comfort of the passengers in an aircraft during flight
- a person whose job is to collect and deliver letters
- person trained to take care of sick or injured people
- skilled work repairing or using machines
- a person who shapes people's hair into a style by cutting, setting, etc.
- a married woman who runs a household
- a person who delivers milk

milkman

housewife

hairdresser

mechanic

postman

air hostess

taxi driver

nurse

policewoman

policeman

Ⅳ Glossary 词汇表

policeman　*n.* 警察

policewoman　*n.* 女警察

taxi driver　出租汽车司机

air hostess　空中小姐

postman　*n.* 邮递员

nurse　*n.* 护士

mechanic　*n.* 机械师
hairdresser　*n.* 理发师
housewife　*n.* 家庭妇女
milkman　*n.* 送牛奶的人

Lesson 9

How are you today?
你今天好吗？

I New words 新单词

1. **hello** *int.* 喂（表示问候）

> hello *int.* 喂（表示问候）
> hallo *int.* 喂，哈啰
> halloa *n. & v.* 喂，啊呀；喊叫

_____, who's speaking, please?

2. **hi** *int.* 喂，嗨

> hi *int.* 喂，嗨（引人注意时的喊声，打招呼）
> heil *int.* 嗨（表示欢迎或欢呼）

_____! Is anybody there?

3. **how** *adv.* 怎样

> how *adv.* 怎样
> how about 怎么样，如何
> what *int.* 怎么，多么；*adj. & pron.* 什么

_____ about playing a game of chess now?

4. **today** *adv.* 今天

> yesterday *adv.* 昨天
> tomorrow *adv.* 明天

What day is it _____?

5. **well** *adj.* 身体好的

> well *adj. & adv.* 身体好的；好，适当地
> unwell *adj.* 身体不好的

He will soon get _____.

6. **fine** *adj.* 美好的

> fine *adj.* 美好的
> nice *adj.* 美好的，和蔼的
> good *adj.* 好的，有益的

That's a _____ thing to say!

7. **thanks** *int.* 谢谢

> thanks *int.* 谢谢
> thank you 谢谢
> thanks to 由于，因为，多亏

It was _____ to John that we won the game.

8. **goodbye** *int.* 再见

> goodbye *int.* 再见
> see you 再见
> bye-bye 再见

We said our _____ to each other and left.

9. **see** *v.* 见

> see *v.* 见
> watch *v.* 看，注视，监视
> look *v.* 看，注视，打量

I can _____ two ships in the harbor.

Ⅱ *Make sentences using the under-mentioned words* 单词造句

hello — how

_____.

hi — well

_____.

fine — thanks

_____.

goodbye — see

_____.

III Match 连线

- used to greet somebody, attract attention, or　see
  express surprise
- used as a greeting　　　　　　　　　　　　　　goodbye
- in what manner or way; in what state or station　thanks
- in good health　　　　　　　　　　　　　　　fine
- of good quality　　　　　　　　　　　　　　　well
- (words expressing) gratefulness　　　　　　　how
- expression used when parting　　　　　　　　hi
- to find; perceive with one's eyes　　　　　　hello

IV Glossary 词汇表

hello　*int.* 喂（表示问候）
hi　*int.* 喂，嗨
how　*adv.* 怎样
today　*adv.* 今天
well　*adj.* 身体好
fine　*adj.* 美好的
thanks　*int.* 谢谢
goodbye　*int.* 再见
see　*v.* 见

Lesson 10

Look at...

看······

1. **fat** *adj.* 胖的

> fat *adj.* 胖的
> plump *adj.* 圆胖的，丰满的
> stout *adj.* 矮胖的

Her father is too _____ to play handball.

2. **woman** *n.* 女人

> woman *n.* 女人
> female *n. & adj.* 女性；妇女的
> girl *n.* 女孩
> womanlike *adj.* 女人般地

It's more than a _____ can tolerate.

3. **thin** *adj.* 瘦的

> thin *adj.* 瘦的
> fleshless *adj.* 瘦的，消瘦的
> slim *adj.* 瘦的，苗条的

You should eat more; you're too _____ .

4. **tall** *adj.* 高的

tall   *adj.* 高的
high   *adj.* 高的，高原的，高等的，高尚的
tallness   *n.* 高，高度

He is 1 meter 80 centimeters _____.

5. **short**   *adj.* 矮的

short   *adj.* 矮的
shorty   *n.* 矮个子
chunky   *adj.* 矮矮胖胖的

The _____ boy is my son.

6. **dirty**   *adj.* 脏的

dirty   *adj.* 脏的
dirty word   脏字
miry   *adj.* 泥泞的

His feet left _____ marks all over the floor.

7. **clean**   *adj.* 干净的

clean   *adj.* 干净的
cleanly   *adj. & adv.* 干净的，清洁地
fair   *adj.* 干净的，美丽的，（天气）晴朗的
neatly   *adv.* 干净地

Boys, are your hands _____?

8. **hot**   *adj.* 热的

hot   *adj.* 热的
warm   *adj. & v.* 暖和的；温暖
fever   *n.* 发热，发烧
heat   *n. & v.* 热；加热

Here is some _____ tea for you.

9. **cold** *adj.* 冷的

> cold *adj.* 冷的
> cool *adj.* 凉爽的
> cold sweat 冷汗

I'd prefer a _____ drink.

10. **old** *adj.* 老的

> old *adj.* 老的
> aged *adj.* 年老的
> gray *adj.* 灰白的，老的
> outdated *adj.* 老式的，过时的

How _____ are you?

11. **young** *adj.* 年轻的

> young *adj.* 年轻的
> youthy *adj.* 年轻的，少壮的
> youthful *adj.* 年轻的，青年的

He is _____ for his age.

12. **busy** *adj.* 忙的

> busy *adj.* 忙的
> hurry *n. & v.* 匆忙；加速
> busily *adv.* 忙碌地
> fuss *n.* 忙乱

Don't bother me! I'm _____.

13. **lazy** *adj.* 懒的

> lazy *adj.* 懒的
> idle *adj.* 懒惰的，无用的，游手好闲的
> lazybones *n.* 懒骨头

He is not stupid, just _____.

II Make sentences using the under-mentioned words 单词造句

fat — old

_____.

woman — clean

_____.

thin — young

_____.

tall — short

_____.

dirty — hot

_____.

cold — hot

_____.

busy — lazy

_____.

III Match 连线

- overweight; thick; having excessive fat in the body
- feminine adult; women in general
- lean; not plump;
- of great or specific height
- having little space or time; inadequate
- not clean; soiled; dull in color
- no dirt or impurities; not soiled or used
- very much above usual temperature
- low temperature

young
busy
lazy
old
cold
hot
clean
dirty
short

- aged; not new   tall
- youthful; only in existence for a short period of time   thin
- having a lot of work to do; with many activities   woman
- not willing or doing little work   fat

IV Glossary 词汇表

fat   *adj.* 胖的

woman   *n.* 女人

thin   *adj.* 瘦的

tall   *adj.* 高的

short   *adj.* 矮的

dirty   *adj.* 脏的

clean   *adj.* 干净的

hot   *adj.* 热的

cold   *adj.* 冷的

old   *adj.* 老的

young   *adj.* 年轻的

busy   *adj.* 忙的

lazy   *adj.* 懒的

Lesson 11

Is this your shirt?
这是你的衬衫吗？

I New words 新单词

1. **whose** *pron.* 谁的

> whose *pron.* 谁的
> who *pron.* 谁（主格）
> whom *pron.* 谁（宾格）

_____ bicycle is this?

2. **blue** *adj.* 蓝色的

> blue *adj.* 蓝色的
> blueness *n.* 蓝色，蓝，青
> blue eye 蓝眼睛
> blueprint 蓝图

Your hands are _____ with cold.

3. **perhaps** *adv.* 大概

> perhaps *adv.* 大概
> maybe *adv.* 大概，或许
> probably *adv.* 大概，或许

_____ the letter will come today.

4. **white** *adj.* 白色的

> white   *adj.* 白色的
> white-collar   *adj.* 白领阶层的，脑力劳动者的
> white-faced   *adj.* 面容苍白的，前额有白斑的
> white-haired   *adj.* 长着白发的，被捧场的
> white-lipped   *adj.* 嘴唇发白的

The eggs are _____.

5. **catch**   *v.* 抓住

> catch   *v.* 抓住
> catch hold of   抓住
> seize   *v.* 抓住，夺取

The cat _____ mice.

Ⅱ Make sentences using the under-mentioned words 单词造句

blue — like

_____.

whose — white

_____.

perhaps — catch

_____.

Ⅲ Match 连线

- with the color of a cloudless sky   catch
- of whom; of which   white
- possibly; probably   perhaps
- a very light color, like snow or common salt   whose
- get by hunting; trap   blue

Ⅳ Glossary 词汇表

whose   *pron.* 谁的
blue   *adj.* 蓝色的
perhaps   *adv.* 大概
white   *adj.* 白色的
catch   *v.* 抓住

Whose is this...? This is my/ your / his / her... 这……是谁 的？这是我的 / 你的 / 他的 / 她 的……

Whose is that...? That is my/your / his / her... 那……是谁的？那是我的 / 你的 / 他的 / 她的……

I New words 新单词

1. **father** *n.* 父亲

> father   *n.* 父亲
> Father's Day   父亲节
> father-in-law   *n.* 岳父
> dad   *n.* 爸爸

Is that your _____ ?

2. **mother** *n.* 母亲

> mother   *n.* 母亲
> Mother's Day   母亲节
> motherlike   *adj.* 母亲似的
> mom   *n.* 妈妈

My _____ is a teacher.

3. **blouse** *n.* 女衬衫

> blouse   *n.* 女衬衫
> shirt   *n.* 衬衫，衬衣（通常指男的）
> skirt   *n.* 裙子
> blouson   夹克衫，松紧带束腰的女衫

This _____ suits you very well.

4. **sister**   *n.* 姐，妹

> sister   *n.* 姐，妹
> sisterhood   *n.* 姐妹关系
> sisterly   *adj.* 姐妹一般的
> sister-german   *n.* 亲姐妹
> sister-in-law   *n.* 夫或妻的姊妹

She has been like a _____ to me.

5. **tie**   *n.* 领带

> tie   *n.* 领带
> tiepin   *n.* 领带别针
> necktie   *n.* 领带

He wears a grey _____ today.

6. **brother**   *n.* 兄，弟

> brother   *n.* 兄，弟
> brotherhood   *n.* 手足情谊，兄弟关系
> brotherless   *adj.* 无兄弟的
> brotherly   *adj.* 兄弟的，亲兄弟般的，亲切的，充
>   满情谊的

We must all stand together, _____ !

7. **his**   *pron. & adj.*   他的

> his   *pron. & adj.* 他的
> he   *pron.* 他（主格）
> him   *pron.* 他（宾格）

If you can't find your hat, take _____ .

8. **her** *pron. & adj.* 她的

> her *pron. & adj.* 她的
> hers *pron.* 她的
> she *pron.* 她（主格）

This letter is addressed to _____ .

II Make sentences using the under-mentioned words 单词造句

father — brother

_____ .

mother — sister

_____ .

blouse — her

_____ .

tie — his

_____ .

III Match 连线

- male parent   her
- female parent   his
- large garment worn by women on the upper part of   brother
  the body
- a female who has the same parents as someone else   tie
- necktie   sister
- a male having at least one parent in common with the   blouse
  other person
- belonging to him   mother
- belonging to her   father

Ⅳ Glossary 词汇表

father   *n.* 父亲

mother   *n.* 母亲

blouse   *n.* 女衬衫

sister   *n.* 姐，妹

tie   *n.* 领带

brother   *n.* 兄，弟

his   *pron. & adj.* 他的

her   *pron. & adj.* 她的

13 A new dress
一件新连衣裙

I New words 新单词

1. **colour** *n.* 颜色

colour *n.* 颜色
off-colour *adj.* 颜色不佳的
light-coloured *adj.* 浅色的
colour-blind *adj.* 色盲的
tinct *n.* 颜色，燃料，色泽

There isn't enough _____ in the picture.

2. **green** *adj.* 绿色的

green *adj.* 绿色的
greenness *n.* 绿色，未熟，新鲜
greenly *adv.* 绿色地
greenbelt *n.* 绿色地带

She was dressed in _____.

3. **come** *v.* 来

come *v.* 来
coming *n.* 来到
go *v.* 去

The children _____ reluctantly when I insisted.

4. **upstairs**   *adv.* 楼上

> upstairs   *adv.* 楼上
> stairway   *n.* 楼梯
> downstairs   *adv.* 楼下

The bathroom is _____.

5. **smart**   *adj.* 漂亮的，时髦的

> smart   *adj.* 漂亮的，时髦的
> modern   *adj.* 时髦的，现代的
> fashionable   *adj.* 时髦的，流行的

She always wears _____ clothes.

6. **hat**   *n.* 帽子

> hat   *n.* 帽子
> hatter   *n.* 帽子制造者
> cap   *n.* 帽子，军帽，笔帽，瓶帽

A _____ is a covering for the head, especially one with a shaped crown and brim..

7. **same**   *adj.* 相同的

> same   *adj.* 相同的
> sameness   *n.* 同一，一致性
> similar   *adj.* 相似的，类似的
> different   *adj.* 不同的

Thank you all the _____.

8. **lovely**   *adj.* 可爱的，秀美动人的

> lovely   *adj.* 可爱的，秀美动人的
> loveliness   *n.* 可爱

> cute   *adj.* 可爱的，伶俐的
> likeable   *adj.* 可爱的

The house has many large rooms and there is a _____ garden.

II Make sentences using the under-mentioned words 单词造句

colour — green

_____.

come — upstairs

_____.

smart — hat

_____.

same — lovely

_____.

III Match 连线

- visible quality that objects have, produced by rays of light of different wavelengths being reflected by them   lovely

- of the colour between blue and yellow in the spectrum   same

- go towards a person, a place or a position   hat

- to or on a higher floor; of the upper floors   smart

- stylish; fashionable   upstairs

- covering for the head   come

- not different, unchanged   green

- beautiful, attractive   colour

IV Glossary 词汇表

colour   *n.* 颜色

green   *adj.* 绿色的

come   *v.* 来

upstairs   *adv.* 楼上

smart   *adj.* 漂亮的，时髦的

hat   *n.* 帽子

same   *adj.* 相同的

lovely   *adj.* 可爱的，秀美动人的

What colour is your...?
你的……是什么颜色的?

I New words 新单词 ....

1. **case** *n.* 箱子

case	*n.*	箱子
box	*n.*	盒子，箱，包厢
trunk	*n.*	箱子，躯干，树干
chest	*n.*	箱，柜，胸腔

She takes a _____ full of clothes with her.

2. **carpet** *n.* 地毯

carpet	*n.*	地毯
carpeting	*n.*	毛毯，地毡毛毯
footcloth	*n.*	地毯
rug	*n.*	小地毯，垫子

The _____ won't double up.

3. **dog** *n.* 狗

dog	*n.*	狗
doggie	*n.*	小狗
dog skin		狗皮
Pekinese	*n.*	哈巴狗

Some people keep _____ in their houses.

II Make sentences using the under-mentioned words 单词造句

case — clothes

_____.

carpet — dog

_____.

III Match 连线

- container or box that can store things
- sewn or other fabric which is put on the surface of the floor
- four-footed animal related to the wolf and jackal which any people keep as pets

dog

case

carpet

IV Glossary 词汇表

case　　*n.* 箱子

carpet　*n.* 地毯

dog　　*n.* 狗

Lesson 15

Your passports, please.
请出示你们的护照。

Ⅰ New words 新单词

1. customs *n.* 海关

> customs *n.* 海关
> customs inspection 海关检查
> customs agreement 海关协定
> customs area 海关境界
> customs bureau 税务局，海关

The spy was stopped at the _____ and questioned.

2. officer *n.* 官员

> officer *n.* 官员
> official *n.* 官员，公务员
> official position 官职

His father is a law _____.

3. girl *n.* 女孩，姑娘

> girl *n.* 女孩，姑娘
> woman *n.* 妇女，女人
> lady *n.* 夫人，女士

The little _____ is ill.

4. Danish *adj. & n.* 丹麦的；丹麦人

> Danish   *adj. & n.* 丹麦的；丹麦人
> Denmark   *n.* 丹麦

Andersen is a _____ writer.

5. **friend**   *n.* 朋友

> friend   *n.* 朋友
> friendly   *adj.* 友好的，友谊的
> friendless   *adj.* 没有朋友的，无依无靠的
> friendliness   *n.* 友谊，友善，亲切，亲密
> friendship   *n.* 友谊，友好

A _____ in need is a friend indeed.

6. **Norwegian**   *adj. & n.* 挪威的；挪威人

> Norwegian   *adj. & n.* 挪威的；挪威人
> Norway   *n.* 挪威

Have you ever heard the popular song "_____ Wood"?

7. **passport**   *n.* 护照

> passport   *n.* 护照
> passport barrier   出国限制（某些国家在签发出国护照时所加的障碍）

Do you have a British _____?

8. **brown**   *adj.* 棕色的

> brown   *adj.* 棕色的
> brown race   棕色皮肤人种
> brown body   褐色体
> brown bread   黑面包

She has a pair of dark _____ shoes.

9. **tourist**   *n.* 旅游者

tourist   *n.* 旅游者
visitor   *n.* 访问者，来宾，游客
traveler   *n.* 旅行者
tourist agency   旅行社
tourist attraction   游览胜地
tourist car   游览车

The Great Wall draws millions of _____ every year.

II Make sentences using the under-mentioned words 单词造句

customs — tourist

_____.

officer — passport

_____.

girl — brown

_____.

danish — friend

_____.

norwegian — tourist

_____.

III Match 连线

- government department that collects taxes   tourist
- person who holds a position of authority in a business or government   brown
- a female child; an unmarried young woman   passport
- of Denmark and the Danes   Norwegian
- person, who one knows, trusts and feel affection for   friend

- people of the country of Norway   Danish
- official document authorizing a person to travel   girl
  abroad
- of a colour lighter than red but darker than yellow   officer
- one who is traveling for fun   customs

IV Glossary 词汇表

customs   *n.* 海关

officer   *n.* 官员

girl   *n.* 女孩，姑娘

Danish   *adj. & n.* 丹麦的；丹麦人

friend   *n.* 朋友

Norwegian   *adj. & n.* 挪威的；挪威人

passport   *n.* 护照

brown   *adj.* 棕色的

tourist   *n.* 旅游者

Are you...?

你是……吗？

I New words 新单词 ....

1. **Russian** *adj. & n.* 俄罗斯的；俄罗斯人

> Russian *adj. & n.* 俄罗斯的；俄罗斯人
> Russia *n.* 俄国，俄罗斯

Are you _____?

2. **Dutch** *adj. & n.* 荷兰的；荷兰人

> Dutch *adj. & n.* 荷兰的；荷兰人
> Holland *n.* 荷兰
> Netherlands *n.* 荷兰
> Hollander *n.* 荷兰人，荷兰船
> Netherlander *n.* 荷兰人

_____ means people from Netherlands.

3. **these** *pron.* 这些（this 的复数）

> these *pron.* 这些（this 的复数）
> those *pron.* 那些（that 的复数）
> this *pron.* 这
> that *pron.* 那

Come here and look at _____ pictures.

4. **red** *adj.* 红色的

> red　*adj.* 红色的
> redness　*n.* 红，红色
> red-blind　*n.* 红色盲
> red-eyed　*adj.* 红眼的，眼圈哭红的

Her face is _____ with embarrassment.

5. **grey** *adj.* 灰色的

> grey　*adj.* 灰色的
> gray　*adj.* 灰色的，苍白的
> ashen　*adj.* 灰色的，苍白的
> gray-faced　*adj.* 面色灰白的，面露倦容的

She is dressed in _____.

6. **yellow** *adj.* 黄色的

> yellow　*adj.* 黄色的
> yellowness　*n.* 黄色
> yellow book　黄皮书
> yellow cake　鸡蛋糕

It was autumn and the leaves were beginning to _____.

7. **black** *adj.* 黑色的

> black　*adj.* 黑色的
> dark　*adj.* 黑色的，黑暗的
> black-eyed　*adj.* 黑眼珠的，黑眼圈的
> black-faced　*adj.* 黑面的，有忧色的

He likes _____ coffee.

8. **orange** *adj.* 橘黄色的

orange	*adj.*	橘黄色的
orangery	*n.*	橘园
orange juice		橘子汁

I like this _____ scarf very much.

Ⅱ Make sentences using the under-mentioned words 单词造句

russian — Dutch

_____.

these — red

_____.

grey — black

_____.

yellow — orange

_____.

Ⅲ Match 连线

- person from Russia   orange
- the people or the language of the Netherlands   black
- plural of this   yellow
- having the color of fresh blood   grey
- of the color between black and white   red
- color of butter and ripe lemons   these
- of the darkest color, like coal and is unable to   Dutch
  reflect light
- reddish-yellow   Russian

Ⅳ Glossary 词汇表

Russian　*adj. & n.*　俄罗斯的；俄罗斯人

Dutch　*adj. & n.*　荷兰的；荷兰人

these　*pron.*　这些（this 的复数）

red　*adj.*　红色的

grey　*adj.*　灰色的

yellow　*adj.*　黄色的

black　*adj.*　黑色的

orange　*adj.*　橘黄色的

Lesson 17

How do you do?

你好!

1. **employee** *n.* 雇员

> employee *n.* 雇员
> employer *n.* 雇主
> employ *v. & n.* 雇用，用，使用；雇用
> employment *n.* 雇用，使用，利用，工作，职业

There are 30 _____ in his firm.

2. **hard-working** *adj.* 勤奋的

> hard-working *adj.* 勤奋的
> industrious *adj.* 勤奋的，勤劳的
> diligent *adj.* 勤奋的
> hard-earned *adj.* 辛苦得到的

Though he's not clever, he's a _____ worker and has often done well in the examinations.

3. **sales reps** 推销员

> sales reps 推销员
> salesman *n.* 售货员，推销员
> bagman *n.* 推销员，（贿赂事件的）中间人
> sales promotion 促销
> sales policy 销售方针

· 66 ·

When _____ are sent to different parts of the city, they have to drive in order to carry their products.

4. **man**   *n.* 男人

> man   *n.* 男人
> boy   *n.* 男孩
> gentleman   *n.*. 绅士，先生

A tone of menace entered into the _____'s voice.

5. **office**   *n.* 办公室

> office   *n.* 办公室
> office work   办公室工作
> office worker   办公室人员
> office chair   办公椅

She works in an _____.

6. **assistant**   *n.* 助手

> assistant   *n.* 助手
> helper   *n.* 帮忙者，助手
> assist   *v.* 援助，帮助
> assistance   *n.* 协助，援助，补助，＜英＞国家补助
> office assistant   指办公室干杂务的工作人员

He became an _____ cook after he graduated from the technological school.

Ⅱ *Make sentences using the under-mentioned words* 单词造句

employee — hard-working

_____.

sales reps — man

_____.

office — assistant

_____.

Ⅲ Match 连线 ....

- one who works for another   assistant
- working with care and energy   office
- salesman   man
- adult male human being   sales reps
- position of authority, esp. in a government   hard-working
- helper   employee

Ⅳ Glossary 词汇表 ....

employee   *n.* 雇员
hard-working   *adj.* 勤奋的
sales reps   推销员
man   *n.* 男人
office   *n.* 办公室
assistant   *n.* 助手

Lesson 18

Tired and thirsty
又累又渴

I New words 新单词

1. **matter** *n.* 事情

> matter   *n.* 事情
>
> business   *n.* 事情，事物，商业
>
> matter of fact   事实
>
> matter of course   *n.* 必然发生之事

I have an important _____ to talk to you about.

2. **children** *n.* 孩子们（child 的复数）

> children   *n.* 孩子们（child 的复数）
>
> child   *n.* 孩子
>
> Children's Day   *n.* 儿童节

They have three _____.

3. **tired** *adj.* 累，疲乏

> tired   *adj.* 累，疲乏
>
> weary   *adj.* 疲倦的
>
> tiredness   *n.* 疲劳，疲倦
>
> tireless   *adj.* 不疲劳的

He was too _____ to go any further.

4. **boy** *n.* 男孩

> boy　*n.* 男孩
> man　*n.* 男人
> boyfriend　*n.* 男朋友

The newspaper _____ has delivered the Sunday paper.

5. **thirsty** *adj.* 渴

> thirsty　*adj.* 渴
> thirst　*n.* 渴，口渴
> thirst for　渴望，热望
> thirstily　*adv.* 如饥似渴地
> thirstless　*adj.* 不渴的

I often feel _____ when it's very hot.

6. **mum** *n.* 妈妈（儿语）

> mum　*n.* 妈妈（儿语）
> mom　*n.* 妈妈
> mama　*n.* 妈妈
> mother　*n.* 母亲，妈妈

What are you doing, _____?

7. **sit down** 坐下

> sit down　坐下
> stand up　站起来

_____ , if you please.

8. **right** *adj.* 好，可以

> right　*adj.* 好，可以
> good　*adj.* 好的，有益的，优良的
> fine　*adj.* 美好的，精美的，杰出的

Do you feel all _____?

9. **ice cream** 冰淇淋

> ice cream 冰淇淋
> ice cream cabinet 冰淇淋保藏柜
> ice cream cone 冰淇淋蛋卷
> ice cream powder 冰淇淋粉

I just had dinner and now I want some _____ for dessert.

II Make sentences using the under-mentioned words 单词造句

matter — right

_____.

children — ice cream

_____.

tired — mum

_____.

boy — thirsty

_____.

tired — sit down

_____.

III Match 连线

- specified substance, material, or things   ice cream
- plural of child   right
- feeling that one would like to sleep or rest   sit down
- male child   mum
- having or causing thirst   thirsty
- mother   boy
- rest or fix in some place   tired

- morally good   children
- a sweet frozen food that is made of milk   matter
  products

Ⅳ *Glossary* 词汇表

matter   *n.* 事情

children   *n.* 孩子们（child 的复数）

tired   *adj.* 累，疲乏

boy   *n.* 男孩

thirsty   *adj.* 渴

mum   *n.* 妈妈（儿语）

sit down 坐下

right   *adj.* 好，可以

ice cream 冰淇淋

Look at them!
看看他们／它们！

I New words 新单词

1. **big** *adj.* 大的

> big *adj.* 大的
> large *adj.* 巨大的，宽大的
> great *adj.* 伟大的，重大的

She's a _____ name in the painting world.

2. **small** *adj.* 小的

> small *adj.* 小的
> small-scale 小规模
> small-town *adj.* 褊狭的，小都市的，土里土气的

This is just a _____ matter.

3. **open** *adj.* 开着的

> open *adj.* 开着的
> open-air *adj.* 户外的，野外的
> open-door *adj.* 公开的，（对外关系上）门户开
> 放的

The store is _____.

4. **shut** *adj.* 关着的

> shut away 关起来
> shut off 关掉，切断

> shut out　关在外面，遮住，排除，使不能得分
> shut to　关上

You'd better keep your mouth _____ .

5. **light** *adj.* 轻的

> light　*adj.* 轻的
> light-colored　*adj.* 颜色浅的，不黑的
> light-duty　*adj.* 轻型的
> light-foot　*adj.* 脚步轻捷的
> light-hearted　*adj.* 轻松的，无忧无虑的

The basket is very _____ , and I can easily pick it up.

6. **heavy** *adj.* 重的

> heavy　*adj.* 重的
> heavy-duty　*adj.* 重型的，结实或耐受力强的
> heavy-hearted　*adj.* 心情沉重的

I've had a _____ day.

7. **long** *adj.* 长的

> long　*adj.* 长的
> long-distance　*adj.* <美>长途的，长距离的
> long-distance bus　*n.* 长途汽车
> long-distance call　长途电话
> long-lived　*adj.* 长命的

They talked all night _____ .

8. **shoe** *n.* 鞋子

> shoe　*n.* 鞋子
> shoe-maker　*n.* 鞋匠
> shoeblack　*n.* 擦皮鞋的人
> shoebrush　*n.* 鞋刷

She bought a pair of black _____ last week.

9. **grandfather** *n.* 祖父，外祖父

> grandfather　*n.* 祖父，外祖父
> grand-dad　*n.* 祖父，外祖父
> grandpa　*n.* 爷爷
> grandfatherly　*adj.* 祖父似的，慈祥的

My _____ is already 82.

10. **grandmother** *n.* 祖母；外祖母

> grandmother　*n.* 祖母，外祖母
> grandma　*n.* 祖母，外祖母
> grandmotherly　*adj.* 祖母的

His _____ passed away last year.

II Make sentences using the under-mentioned words 单词造句

big — heavy

_____.

small — light

_____.

open — shut

_____.

long — grandfather

_____.

shoe — grandmother

_____.

III Match 连线

- large in size, number, quantity or extent
- not large or great

grandmother
grandfather

- capable of being entered   shoe
- close; fold together   long
- not heavy; easy to move or lift   heavy
- having great weight   light
- of great or specified length   shut
- outer protection for a person's foot   open
- male grandparent   small
- female grandparent   big

Ⅳ Glossary 词汇表

big　*adj.* 大的

small　*adj.* 小的

open　*adj.* 开着的

shut　*adj.* 关着的

light　*adj.* 轻的

heavy　*adj.* 重的

long　*adj.* 长的

shoe　*n.* 鞋子

grandfather　*n.* 祖父，外祖父

grandmother　*n.* 祖母，外祖母

Lesson 20 Which book?

哪一本书？

1. **give** *v.* 给

> give   *v.* 给
> give a talk 做一次演讲
> give advice 提建议
> take   *v.* 取，拿
> give sb. sth.（ = give sth. to sb.）把……给……

Can you _____ me a book?

2. **one** *pron.* 一个

> one   *pron.* 一个
> one by one 一个接一个
> singly   *adv.* 单个地，一个一个地
> single   *adj.* 单一的，单个的，单独的

_____ or other of us will go there.

3. **which** *question word* 哪一个

> which *question word* 哪一个
> where question word 哪里
> what question word 在哪一方面

_____ child knows the answer?

II Make sentences using the under-mentioned words 单词造句

give — book

_____

one — which?

_____.

III Match 连线

- to cause to receive or have   one
- single thing or person   which
- thing being referred to   give

IV Glossary 词汇表

give   _v._ 给

one   _pron._ 一个

which _question word_ 哪一个

Give me / him / her / us /
them a...

给我／他／她／我们／他们……

Which one? 哪一……?

I New words 新单词

1. **empty** *adj.* 空的

   | empty *adj.* 空的 |
   | bare *adj.* 空的，无遮藏的 |
   | vacant *adj.* 空的，空缺的，空白的 |

   The house is _____ , no one is living there.

2. **full** *adj.* 满的

   | full *adj.* 满的 |
   | expire *adj.* 期满的，届满的 |
   | fill *v.* 装满，充满 |

   Her eyes are _____ of tears.

3. **large** *adj.* 大的

   | large *adj.* 大的，巨大的 |
   | big *adj.* 大的，重大的 |
   | great *adj.* 伟大的 |

   Do you want the _____ size, or the small size?

4. **little** *adj.* 小的

> little *adj.* 小的
> small *adj.* 小的，少的
> tiny *adj.* 很少的，微小的

She is a lovely _____ girl.

5. **small** *adj.* 小的

> small *adj.* 小的
> smaller *adj.* 小的（比较级）
> smallest *adj.* 最小的

The _____ one is yours.

6. **big** *adj.* 大的

> big *adj.* 大的
> bigger *adj.* 较大的
> biggest *adj.* 最大的

It is a _____ ball.

7. **sharp** *adj.* 尖的，锋利的

> sharp *adj.* 尖的，锋利的
> knife-edged *adj.* 锋利的，（声音）尖的
> sharp-cut *adj.* 锋利的，鲜明的
> sharp-angled *adj.* 尖角的

The shears aren't _____ enough to cut the grass.

8. **blunt** *adj.* 钝的

> blunt *adj.* 钝的
> blunt angle 钝角
> blunt tool 钝工具
> blunted edge 钝边
> bluntness *n.* 率直，迟钝

A _____ knife draws no blood.

9. **box**   *n.* 盒子，箱子

> box   *n.* 盒子，箱子（复数形式：boxes）
> case   *n.* 箱子，行李箱，案件
> trunk *n.* 箱子，车厢

I have a mail _____ beside the front door.

10. **glass**   *n.* 杯子

> glass   *n.* 杯子，玻璃杯或有脚的玻璃杯（复数
>   形式：glasses）
> glass-hard   *adj.* 有最高硬度的
> glass bottle   玻璃瓶
> glass brick   （压制）玻璃砖
> glass bulb   玻璃灯泡

I'd like to have a _____ of water.

11. **cup**   *n.* 茶杯

> cup   *n.* 茶杯
> cup-shaped   *adj.* 杯状的
> cup-tie   *n.* 优胜杯决赛
> cup and can   形影不离，亲密的朋友
> cup cake   杯形糕饼，（用杯状容器烤成的）小
>   糕饼

I have a beautiful set of tea _____.

12. **bottle**   *n.* 瓶子

> bottle   *n.* 瓶子
> bottled   *adj.* 瓶装的
> bottleneck   *n.* 瓶颈

There is a _____ of milk on the table.

13. **tin**　*n.* 罐头

> tin　*n.* 罐头
> can　*n.* 罐头，铁罐
> tinner　*n.* 罐头商

He opened a _____ of stew and ate completely.

14. **knife**　*n.* 刀子

> knife　*n.* 刀子
> sword　*n.* 刀，剑
> weapon　*n.* 兵器
> knife rest　刀架
> knifepoint　*n.* 刀尖

Please give me the kitchen _____.

15. **fork**　*n.* 叉子

> fork　*n.* 叉子
> forked　*adj.* 叉状的
> forklift　*n.* 叉式升降机

We use a _____ to eat food.

16. **spoon**　*n.* 勺子

> spoon　*n.* 勺子
> scoop　*n.* 铲子，圆形小勺
> spooner　*n.* 茶匙盘
> spoonful　*n.* 一匙

Please add a _____ of sugar to my coffee.

Ⅱ *Make sentences using the under-mentioned words* 单词造句

blunt — knife

_____.

sharp — fork

_____.

little — tin

_____.

large — box

_____.

full — glass

_____.

empty — cup

_____.

bottle — spoon

_____.

III Match 连线

- not sharp; dull or slow in understanding
- something that has a fine cutting edge
- not big; short
- of great size or extent
- complete or entire
- containing nothing
- container with a plain and gentle bottom
- a hard transparent substance produced by fusion used for windows, bottles
- a container usually for water, with a handle at the side
- narrow-necked glass or plastic container, with an opening which can be closed
- sealed container for preserving food
- cutting instrument with a sharp blade and handle

spoon
fork
knife
tin
bottle
cup
glass
box
empty
full
large
little

- a tool with prongs for holding food   sharp
- device which is used to eat with or stir liquids or   blunt
  other soft food

IV Glossary 词汇表

empty   *adj.* 空的

full   *adj.* 满的

large   *adj.* 大的

little   *adj.* 小的

small   *adj.* 小的

big   *adj.* 大的

sharp   *adj.* 尖的，锋利的

blunt   *adj.* 钝的

box   *n.* 盒子，箱子

glass   *n.* 杯子

cup   *n.* 茶杯

bottle   *n.* 瓶子

tin   *n.* 罐头

knife   *n.* 刀子

fork   *n.* 叉子

spoon   *n.* 勺子

Lesson 22

Which glasses?
哪几只杯子？

I New words 新单词

1. **on**　*prep.* 在……之上

> on　*prep.* 在……之上
> up　*prep.* 在上，向上
> top　*n. & v.* 上部
> upside　*n.* 上边，上部
> above　*prep. & adj. & adv.* 在……上方；上面的；
> 　上述地

He stood _____ the cliff top looking out to the sea.

2. **shelf**　*n.* 架子，搁板

> shelf　*n.* 架子，搁板
> stand　*n.* 架子，看台，台
> frame　*n.* 框架，支架
> rack　*n.* 行李架
> shelf list　书架目录，排架目录

He took the cup off the _____.

II Make sentences using the under-mentioned words 单词造句

on — shelf

_____.

III Match 连线

shelf

- towards; close to
- a flat piece of wood, metal, glass etc. that people   on

  put books and other things on

IV Glossary 词汇表

> on   *prep.* 在……之上
>
> shelf   *n.* 架子，搁板

Lesson 23

Give me / him / her / us / them some... 给我 / 他 / 她 / 我们 / 他们一些……
Which one? 哪些?

I New words 新单词

1. **desk**   *n.* 课桌

> desk   *n.* 课桌，书桌，写字台，办公桌
> desk keyboard   桌式控制台
> desk lamp   桌灯
> deskmate   同坐一张课桌的学生
> deskwork   *n.* 案头工作，文书工作

He is working at his _____.

2. **table**   *n.* 桌子

> table   *n.* 桌子，餐桌，会议桌，工作台，手术台
> table-board   *n.* 牌桌，桌面，台面，包饭
> table-tennis   *n.* 桌球
> table cloth   桌布

They sat round the _____ and made this big decision.

3. **plate**   *n.* 盘子

> plate   *n.* 盘子
> plate-basket   *n.* 餐具篮

> plate-rack   *n.* 餐具盘
>
> dishware   *n.* 碟，餐具，盘

I'd like to order a _____ of spaghetti.

4. **cupboard**   *n.* 食橱

> cupboard   *n.* 食橱
>
> cupboard button   旋扣
>
> cupboard proofer   橱柜式检验台
>
> cabinet   *n.* 储藏柜

Please take the plates and bowls from the _____.

5. **cigarette**   *n.* 香烟

> cigarette   *n.* 香烟
>
> cigar   *n.* 雪茄
>
> smoke   *n.* 烟，烟尘；*v.* 抽烟，吸烟
>
> tobacco   *n.* 烟草，烟草制品

He lights a _____ to calm his nerves.

6. **television**   *n.* 电视机

> television   *n.* 电视机
>
> television camera   电视摄像机
>
> television station   电视台
>
> television network   电视广播公司

What's on _____ tonight?

7. **floor**   *n.* 地板

> floor   *n.* 地板
>
> flooring   *n.* 地板材料
>
> hatchway   *n.* 舱口，地板，天花板出入口
>
> on the floor   在地上

We live on the third _____.

8. **dressing table**　梳妆台

> dressing table　梳妆台
>
> dresser　*n.* 梳妆台，化妆师
>
> wash and dress　梳洗

Do you have a _____ in your living room?

9. **magazine**　*n.* 杂志

> magazine　*n.* 杂志
>
> journal　*n.* 定期刊物，杂志
>
> magazine advertising　杂志广告
>
> magazinist　*n.* 杂志（或期刊）编辑，杂志（或期刊）出版商

I buy several _____ every month.

10. **bed**　*n.* 床

> bed　*n.* 床
>
> go tobed　上床，上床睡觉
>
> bed-sitting-room　*n.* 寝室客厅两用房间
>
> bed board　床板

What time did you go to _____ last night?

11. **newspaper**　*n.* 报纸

> newspaper　*n.* 报纸
>
> newspaper agency　报纸代售处
>
> newspaper boy　报童
>
> newspaper office　报社

He is reading _____.

12. **stereo**　*n.* 立体声音响

> stereo　*n.* 立体声音响
> stereo adapter　立体声附加器（控制装置）
> stereo amplifier　立体声放大器
> stereo broadcasting　立体声广播
> stereo camera　立体摄像机（摄影机）

He is planning to buy a set of _____.

II Make sentences using the under-mentioned words 单词造句

desk — magazine

_____.

table — newspaper

_____.

plate — cupboard

_____.

cigarette — floor

_____.

dressing table — bed

_____.

television — stereo

_____.

III Match 连线

- a flat-topped piece of furniture for writing, reading　　　stereo
- piece of furniture consisting of a flat top supported　　　newspaper
  on one or more legs
- shallow (usu. round) dish made use of china,　　　bed
  from which food is served or eaten
- a storage closet　　　magazine

- a roll or cut tobacco leaves packed by paper for smoking
- transmission of images by radio waves
- the layer of a building; the surface of which covers the ground in a room
- piece of bedroom furniture with a mirror and drawers, used especially by women when they dress, make up, etc.
- periodical publication
- a piece of furniture to sleep or rest
- regular printed, usu. daily or weekly, publication comprising news reports
- stereophonic sound or record-player

dressing
table
floor
television

cigarette

cupboard
plate
table

desk

IV Glossary 词汇表

desk   n. 课桌
table   n. 桌子
plate   n. 盘子
cupboard   n. 食橱
cigarette   n. 香烟
television   n. 电视机
floor   n. 地板
dressing table   梳妆台
magazine   n. 杂志
bed   n. 床
newspaper   n. 报纸
stereo   n. 立体声音响

24

Mrs. Smith's Kitchen
史密斯太太的厨房

I New words 新单词

1. **Mrs**. 夫人

> Mrs. 夫人
>
> madam *n*. 女士，夫人
>
> lady *n*. 女士，夫人，小姐

_____ Taylor has a 7-year-old daughter.

2. **kitchen** *n*. 厨房

> kitchen *n*. 厨房
>
> kitchenware *n*. 厨房用具
>
> kitchen stove 厨灶

There is a stack of dishes to be washed in the _____.

3. **refrigerator** *n*. 电冰箱

> refrigerator *n*. 电冰箱
>
> fridge *n*. 电冰箱
>
> refrigerator car 冷藏车
>
> refrigeratory *adj*. 制冷的；*n*. 冰箱

Our _____ is white.

4. **right** *n*. 右边

> right　*n.* 右边
> right-hand　*adj.* 右手的，得力的
> right-hand bend　右转弯
> on theright　在右边

The school is on the left of the road, and his house is on the

_____ .

5. **electric**　*adj.* 带电的，可通电的

> electric　*adj.* 带电的，可通电的
> electric attraction　电吸引，电引力
> electric bulb　电灯泡
> electric car　电车
> electrical　*adj.* 电的，有关电的
> electricity　*n.* 电流，电，电学

This heavy freighter is driven by two _____ motors.

6. **left**　*n.* 左边

> left　*n.* 左边
> left-hand　*adj.* 左侧的，左手的
> left-hand bend　左转弯
> left-handed　*adj.* 惯用左手的，用左手的
> left-hander　*n.* 左撇子，笨拙，左手投球
> on theleft　在左边

The hospital is on the _____ of the road.

7. **cooker**　*n.* 炉子，炊具

> cooker　*n.* 炉子，炊具
> cook　*n. & v.* 厨师，炊事员；烹调，煮，伪造
> cooking　*n.* 烹饪
> cookery　*n.* 烹调术
> cookery-book　*n.*（＝cookbook）烹饪全书，食谱

We usually use a gas _____ to cook.

8. **middle**   *n.* 中间

> middle   *n.* 中间
> in the middle of   在……之间
> mid   *adj.* 中部的，中间的
> medial   *adj.* 中间的，平均的

Please stand in the _____ of the room.

9. **of**   *prep.* （属于）……的

> of   *prep.* （属于）……的
> belong   *v.* 属于
> attribute   *v.* 属于，归属于，归结于

The wall _____ the garden is White.

10. **room**   *n.* 房间

> room   *n.* 房间
> room service   房间服务部
> house   *n.* 房子，住宅
> home   *n.* 家，家乡，住宅

He is in the next _____.

11. **cup**   *n.* 杯子

> cup   *n.* 杯子
> cup-shaped   *adj.* 杯状的
> cup cake   杯形糕饼，（用杯状容器烤成的）小
>   糕饼
> glass   *n.* 玻璃杯
> bottle   *n.* 瓶子

Would you like a _____ of green tea?

II Make sentences using the under-mentioned words 单词造句

Mrs. — room

_____.

kitchen — cooker

_____.

refrigerator — electric

_____.

right — left

_____.

middle — of

_____.

cup — water

_____.

III Match 连线

- title prefixed to a married woman's name
- room where food is prepared and cooked
- a special cupboard used for refrigerating food or drink by electricity
- of or located on the side of the left
- of something charged with or produced by electricity
- of, on or towards the side of the body which is toward the west when a person faces north
- stove for cooking food
- central; medial
- belong to

cup

room

middle

cooker

left

of

electric

right

refrigerator

- part of house separated by wall, ceiling, floor etc   kitchen
- a container usually for water, with a handle at the   Mrs.
  side

IV Glossary 词汇表

Mrs. 夫人
kitchen *n.* 厨房
refrigerator *n.* 电冰箱
right *n.* 右边
electric *adj.* 带电的，可通电的
left *n.* 左边
cooker *n.* 炉子，炊具
middle *n.* 中间
of *prep.* （属于）……的
room *n.* 房间
cup *n.* 杯子

Where is it?

它在哪里?

New words 新单词

1. **where** *adv.* 在哪里

> where   *adv.* 在哪里
> there   *adv.* 在那里
> here   *adv. & n.* 在这里，此时，这时，[宗] 在尘
> 世间；这里

_____ is the telephone?

2. **in** *prep.* 在……里

> in   *prep.* 在……里
> on   *prep. & adv.* 在……之上，靠近，向，在……
> 时候；在上，向前
> at   *prep.* 在，于，向，对准，在……方面

Come _____ , please!

Make sentences using the under-mentioned words 单词造句

where — in

_____ .

Ⅲ Match 连线

- at or in which place   in
- having as a position or state within   where

Ⅳ Glossary 词汇表

> where   *adv.*   在哪里
>
> in   *prep.*   在……里

Mrs. Smith's living room
史密斯太太的客厅

I New words 新单词

1. **living room** 客厅

living room 客厅
drawing room 客厅，起居室
living space 生存空间，可居住面积
living habit 生活方式（习性）
living cost 生活费用

We have moved into a new flat with one _____ and two bedrooms.

2. **near** *prep.* 靠近

near *prep.* 靠近
nearness *n.* 接近，靠近
close *adj.* 近的，紧密的
near by 在附近，邻近

There is a shopping center _____ our school.

3. **window** *n.* 窗户

window *n.* 窗户
window frame 窗框
window curtain 窗帘
window screening 窗纱

Please shut the _____.

4. **armchair** *n.* 扶手椅

> armchair *n.* 扶手椅
> chair *n.* 椅子

She seated herself in the _____.

5. **door** *n.* 门

> door *n.* 门
> gate *n.* 大门
> gateway *n.* 门，通路，网关
> door lamp 门灯

Will you wait at the _____?

6. **picture** *n.* 图画

> picture *n.* 图画
> drawing *n.* 图画，制图，素描
> picture book 图画书
> painting *n.* 绘画，油画

She drew a _____ of me.

7. **wall** *n.* 墙

> wall *n.* 墙
> wallboard 墙板
> wallpaper *n.* 墙纸
> on the wall 在墙上

We have painted all the _____ white.

Ⅱ *Make sentences using the under-mentioned words* 单词造句

living room — armchair

_____.

near — house

_____ .

window — door

_____ .

picture — wall

_____ .

III Match 连线

- room in a private house for general use during   wall
  the daytime
- with only a short distance or time between   picture
- opening constructed in a wall to let light or air   door
  in and out
- chair with supports for the arms
  armchair
- doorway; movable barrier that closes the   window
  entrance to a building, room, etc.
- drawing, painting or photograph
  living room
- continuous upright solid structure of stone or   near
  wood forming one side of a building

IV Glossary 词汇表

living room 客厅
near *prep.* 靠近
window n. 窗户
armchair *n.* 扶手椅
door *n.* 门
picture *n.* 图画
wall *n.* 墙

Where are they?

它们在哪里?

I New words 新单词

1. **trousers** *n.* 长裤

> trousers   *n.* 长裤
> pants   *n.* 裤子，短裤
> trousers pocket   裤子口袋
> trouser   *adj.* 裤子的
> breeches   *n.* 马裤
> shorts   *n.* 短裤

The _____ go well with my sweater.

II Make sentences using the under-mentioned words 单词造句

trousers — color

_____.

III Match 连线

● an outer garment covering the body from the
waist to the ankles, or sometimes to the knees,
with a separate part fitting over each leg

trousers

IV Glossary 词汇表

trousers   *n.* [复数] 长裤

Lesson 28

Come in, Amy.
进来，艾米。

I New words 新单词

1. **shut** *v.* 关门

> shut *v.* 关门
> shut away 关起来
> shut down （把窗子等）放下关下，[机]（使）
>   机器等关闭，停车
> shut up shop 关店，歇业
> close *v.* 关闭，结束

He decided to _____ down the shop.

2. **bedroom** *n.* 卧室

> bedroom *n.* 卧室
> bed *n.* 床
> bed rest 卧床休养期
> living room 客厅

We have a large _____ and two small ones.

3. **untidy** *adj.* 乱的，不整齐的

> untidy *adj.* 乱的，不整齐的
> tidy *adj.* 整齐的
> disorder *adj.* 杂乱的，混乱的
> chaos *n.* 混乱，混沌

This is an _____ garden, isn't it?

4. **must** *v. & awx.* 必须，应该

> must   *v. & awx.* 必须，应该
> have to   不得不，只好
> should   *v. & aux.* 将要，应该

You _____ not go there alone.

5. **open**   *v.* 打开

> open   *v.* 打开
> unfold   *v.* 打开，显露，呈现
> unclose   *v.* 打开
> unpack   *v.* 打开，揭开

_____ your book at Page twenty-one.

6. **air**   *v.* 使……通风，换换空气

> air   *v.* 使……通风，换换空气
> airiness   *n.* 通风，空虚
> airway   *n.* 通风孔
> air-conditioner   *n.* 空调机
> air-cooler   *n.* 空气冷却器，冷气装置

She _____ the room by opening the window.

7. **put**   *v.* 放置

> put   *v.* 放置
> place   *v. & n.* 放置；地方
> lay   *v.* 放置，铺设，下蛋
> deposit   *v.* 存放，堆积

You seem to have _____ too much salt in this dish.

8. **clothes**   *n.* 衣服

clothes　*n.* 衣服，衣服或者服饰的总称	
garment　*n.* 外衣，衣服	
vesture　*n.* 衣服，罩袍，覆盖	
clothes-line　*n.* 晾衣绳	
clothes-pin　*n.* 衣夹	
clothes rack　衣架	

I like my _____ to be simple but elegant.

9. **wardrobe**　*n.* 衣柜

wardrobe　*n.* 衣柜
chest　*n.* 箱，柜
wardrobe master　剧团的服装管理员
wardrobe mistress　剧团的服装女管理员

I need a larger _____.

10. **dust**　*v.* 掸掉灰尘

dust　*v.* 掸掉灰尘
dust-color　*n.* 灰褐色，暗褐色
dust abatement　除尘
dust arrest　集尘
dust aspirator　吸尘器

_____ yourself down – you're covered in chalk.

11. **sweep**　*v.* 扫

sweep　*v.* 扫
sweep away　一扫而空
sweeping car　扫雪车，扫路车
whisk　*v.* & *n.* 扫，拂；扫帚，毛掸子
besom　*n.* 长扫帚，扫把

He is _____ snow from the steps.

II Make sentences using the under-mentioned words 单词造句

shut — must

_____.

bedroom — untidy

_____.

open — air

_____.

put — clothes

_____.

clothes — wardrobe

_____.

dust — sweep

_____.

III Match 连线

- close; fold together   sweep
- a room for sleeping in (usually at night)   wardrobe
- not tidy; not neat   clothes
- used to express something which is necessary,   air
  urgent, and compulsory
- capable of being entered; not closed   put
- expose to air   dust
- to place   open
- garments for the human body   must
- a cabinet or room designed to keep clothes   untidy
- remove dust   bedroom
- move (dust, etc.) by passing a broom, brush,   shut
  etc., over the surface of something

Ⅳ Glossary 词汇表

shut　*v.* 关门

bedroom　*n.* 卧室

untidy　*adj.* 乱的，不整齐的

must　*v. & awx.* 必须，应该

open　*v.* 打开

air　*v.* 使……通风，换换空气

put　*v.* 放置

clothes　*n.* 衣服

wardrobe　*n.* 衣柜

dust　*v.* 掸掉灰尘

sweep　*v.* 扫

Lesson 29

What must I do?
我应该做什么?

1. **empty** *v.* 倒空，使……变空

> empty *v.* 倒空，使……变空
> emptying *n.* 倒空，空出
> empty-handed *adj.* 空手的，徒手的
> empty-headed 没有头脑

It was raining, and the streets began to _____.

2. **read** *v.* 读

> read *v.* 读
> misread *v.* 读错
> reading *n. & adj.* 阅读，读物；阅读的
> reading book 读本
> reading club 读者俱乐部

He _____ to his children every night.

3. **sharpen** *v.* 削尖，使锋利

> sharpen *v.* 削尖，使锋利
> sharp *adj.* 锐利的，锋利的
> Sharpener *n.* 削刀，磨床，磨器，磨具
> Sharpening 磨快，磨尖，磨刀，削尖，刃
> sharpening stone 磨石

This knife needs _____.

4. **put on** 穿上

> put on   穿上
>
> wear   *v.* 穿,戴
>
> wear out   磨损,用旧
>
> dress   *n. & v.* 女服,童装,服装,衣服;(给……)
> 穿衣

She _____ a coat and goes out.

5. **take off** 脱掉

> take off   脱掉
>
> put off   脱掉,摆脱
>
> take off one's coat   脱大衣,挑衅

She _____ her high-heal shoes _____.

6. **turn on** 开(电灯)

> turn on   开(电灯)
>
> turn on the gas   *v.* 开煤气,打开话匣子
>
> turn-on   *n.* 旋开

Please _____ the radio.

7. **turn off** 关(电灯)

> turn off   关(电灯)
>
> turn-off   *n.* 岔路,支路
>
> close   *v.* 关,关闭
>
> shut   *v.* 关上,关闭

_____ the lights when you leave.

II Make sentences using the under-mentioned words 单词造句

empty — box

_____.

read — book

_____.

sharpen — pencil

_____.

put on — clothes

_____.

take off — coat

_____.

turn on — lamp

_____.

turn off — light

_____.

Ⅲ Match 连线

- make or become empty   turn off
- to study；to understand or comprehend meaning of   turn on
- to make something sharp   take off
- wear   put on
- to remove（especially clothes）   sharpen
- to cause（light, radio, etc.）to operate, esp. by using   read
  a button
- to stop the operation of（a radio, light, etc.）   empty

Ⅳ Glossary 词汇表

empty *v.* 倒空，使……变空
read   *v.* 读

sharpen　*v.* 削尖，使锋利

put on　穿上

take off　脱掉

turn on　开（电灯）

turn off　关（电灯）

Lesson
30

Where's Sally?
萨莉在哪？

1. **garden** *n.* 花园

> garden   *n.* 花园
> garden city   花园城市
> garden architecture   庭园建筑
> garden plot   园地
> gardener   *n.* 园丁

We have only a small _____ .

2. **under**   *prep.* 在……之下

> under   *prep.* 在……之下
> underside   *n.* 下面，下侧
> below   *prep. & adv.* 在……下面；在下，在页底

The dog crept _____ the bed.

3. **tree**   *n.* 树

> tree   *n.* 树
> arbor   *n.* 树，乔木，藤架
> tree breaker   伐树机
> tree cotton   木棉树，从木棉树上制取的纤维
> tree crown   树冠
> tree ring   树木的年轮

We have planted some young _____ in the garden.

4. **climb**   v. 爬，攀登

> climb   v. 爬，攀登
> ascent   n. 上升，攀登
> rock-climbing   n. 攀登岩壁
> climbable   adj. 爬得上去的
> climber   n. 登山者，攀缘植物
> climbing   adj. & n. 攀登的，上升的；攀登

He has _____ to a very high position in his field.

5. **who**   pron. 谁

> who   pron. 谁
> whom   pron. 谁
> whose   pron. 谁的

_____ gave you that book?

6. **run**   v. 跑

> run   v. 跑
> runner   n. 跑步者
> run out   抛出
> runway   跑道
> run over   跑过去
> run after   追逐

The current is _____ strong.

7. **grass**   n. 草，草地

> grass   n. 草，草地
> lawn   n. 草地，草坪
> meadow   n. 草地，牧场
> grass cutter   割草机

> grass farm　牧场，草场
> grass green　草绿色

We sat on the _____ to have our picnic.

8. **after** *prep.* 在……之后

> after *prep.* 在……之后
> back *adv. & adj.* 向后地；后面的
> behind *prep. & adv.* 在……之后；在后
> after a while 不久，过一会儿
> after-dinner *adj.* 正餐后的，晚餐后的

I'll call you _____ I get to the school.

9. **across** *prep.* 横过，穿过

> across *prep.* 横过，穿过
> through *prep. & adj.* 通过，穿过；直达的，直通的
> cross *v.* 横过，通过，交叉
> across country *adv.* 越过田野
> across the way 街对面

We swam _____ the river.

10. **cat** *n.* 猫

> cat *n.* 猫
> catty *adj.* 似猫的，狡猾的，阴险的
> cat's-eye *n.* 猫儿眼，猫眼石
> cat-and-dog *adj.* 吵吵闹闹的，不和的

We've got three _____ and a dog.

Ⅱ *Make sentences using the under-mentioned words* 单词造句

garden — grass

_____.

under — tree

_____.

climb — cat

_____.

who — run

_____.

after — cross

_____.

III Match 连线

- land for growing flowers, vegetables or fruits
- below or beneath
- a tall plant with a wooden trunk and breaches that lives for many years
- to go up towards
- what person or people
- to move with quick steps, to compete in a race or contest
- various kinds of green plants whose blades and stems are eaten by sheep, cows, etc.
- later than; following in time
- from one side to the other
- small gentle meat-eating animal which catches rats and can be kept as a pet

cat
across
after

grass
run
who

climb

tree
under
garden

IV Glossary 词汇表

garden   *n.* 花园

under   *prep.* 在……之下

- tree   *n.* 树
- climb   *v.* 爬，攀登
- who   *pron.* 谁
- run   *v.* 跑
- grass   *n.* 草，草地
- after   *prep.* 在……之后
- across   *prep.* 横过，穿过
- cat   *n.* 猫

Lesson 31

What's he/she/it doing?

他／她／它正在做什么？

I New words 新单词

1. **type** *v.* 打字

> type *v.* 打字
> typing *n.* 打字，键入
> typewrite *v.* 打字，用打字机打
> typewriter *n.* 打字机

This file needs to be _____ again.

2. **letter** *n.* 信

> letter *n.* 信
> envelope *n.* 信封
> lettergram *n.* 信件，电报
> letter box 信箱
> letter carrier 邮递员

The doctor has received lots of thank-you _____.

3. **basket** *n.* 篮子

> basket *n.* 篮子
> basketry *n.* 篮筐，编制工艺
> basketball *n.* 篮球

Marry is carrying a _____ of fruit.

· 117 ·

4. **eat** *v.* 吃

> eat *v.* 吃
>
> eat completely 吃光
>
> eat one's words 食言，取消诺言，认错道歉
>
> eatable *adj.* 可以吃的；*n.* 食物，食品

These biscuits _____ crisp.

5. **bone** *n.* 骨头

> bone *n.* 骨头
>
> bone-deep *adj.* 刻骨的
>
> bone cleaner 剔骨机
>
> bone marrow 骨髓

This fish has a lot of _____ in it.

6. **clean** *v.* 清洗

> clean *v.* 清洗
>
> clean away 清除，擦去
>
> clean down 刷干净
>
> clean house 打扫房屋，内部清洗

Have you _____ the kitchen？

7. **tooth** *n.*（复数 teeth）牙齿

> tooth *n.*（复数 teeth）牙齿
>
> tooth powder 牙粉
>
> toothache *n.* 牙痛
>
> tooth form 齿形，齿廓

The children brush their _____ after every meal.

8. **cook** *v.* 做（饭菜）

> cook   *v.* 做（饭菜）
> cook well   容易煮
> cookbook   *n.* 食谱
> cooked   *adj.* 煮熟的
> cooked meat   熟肉

The beef is not _____ enough.

9. **milk**   *n.* 牛奶

> milk   *n.* 牛奶
> milk beverage   乳制饮料
> milk bread   牛奶面包
> milk cattle   乳畜，奶牛
> milk powder   奶粉

Do you prefer _____ chocolate or plain?

10. **meal**   *n.* 饭，一顿饭

> meal   *n.* 饭，一顿饭
> meal ticket   *n.* ＜美＞餐券，饭票
> mealtime   *n.* 进餐时间
> dinner   *n.* 正餐，宴会

I always enjoy my evening _____.

11. **drink**   *v.* 喝

> drink   *v.* 喝
> drink off   一饮而尽
> drinkable   *adj.* 可饮用的
> drinker   *n.* 喝的人，酒徒
> drinking   *n.* 喝，喝酒

Would you like something to _____?

12. **tap**   *n.* （水）龙头

> tap   *n.* （水）龙头
> tap cock   水管栓
> hydrant   *n.* 消防龙头，消防栓
> faucet   *n.* 龙头，旋塞

Don't leave the _____ running!

II Make sentences using the under-mentioned words 单词造句

type — letter

_____.

basket — clean

_____.

eat — bone

_____.

tooth — milk

_____.

drink — tap

_____.

cook — meal

_____.

III Match 连线

- to typewrite   tap
- written message, usually sent by post   drink
- container made of interwoven flexible material   meal
  that used to hold or carry things
- chew and swallow（food）   milk
- any of the various hard parts which made up the   cook
  frame of a human or animal body

- to make or become clean   tooth
- each of the hard white bony structures in the   clean
  jaws, used in biting and chewing things
- to get the food ready to eat by using heat or fire   bone
- a white liquid produced by women or female   eat
  animals for the feeding of their young
- food taken at one, mostly fixed time   basket
- swallow liquid   letter
- tubular plug with a device for allowing liquid to   type
  flow through it

IV Glossary 词汇表

type   v. 打字

letter   n. 信

basket   n. 篮子

eat   v. 吃

bone   n. 骨头

clean   v. 清洗

tooth   n. (复数 teeth) 牙齿

cook   v. 做（饭菜）

milk   n. 牛奶

meal   n. 饭，一顿饭

drink   v. 喝

tap   n. （水）龙头

Lesson

32

A fine day

晴天

I New words 新单词

1. **day** *n.* 日子

> day　*n.* 日子
> day-by-day　*adj.* 每天的
> day-off　*n.* 休息日
> day-to-day　*adj.* 日常的，逐日的
> day after day　*adv.* (=day by day) 日复一日
> day after night　*adv.* 日以继夜

It hasn't stopped raining for _____.

2. **cloud** *n.* 云

> cloud　*n.* 云
> cloud-built　*adj.* 云一样的，空想的
> cloud-castle　*n.* 空中楼阁，梦想
> cloud cover　云量

The top of the mountain is covered with _____.

3. **sky** *n.* 天空

> sky　*n.* 天空
> sky-blue　*adj.* 天蓝色的，淡蓝色，蔚蓝色的
> sky satellite　宇宙卫星，同步卫星
> skydiving　*n.* 跳伞运动
> in the sky　在空中

After the storm the _____ cleared.

4. **sun** *n.* 太阳

> sun *n.* 太阳
> sunrise *n.* 日出
> sunset *n.* 日落
> sunny *adj.* 阳光充足的，照耀的，快乐的
> sunlight *n.* 日光，阳光，日照

The _____ rose at six o'clock.

5. **shine** *v.* 照耀

> shine *v.* 照耀
> shineless *adj.* 无光泽的
> shine in 照射进来
> shine out 照射出去

The water is _____ in the sunlight.

6. **with** *prep.* 和……在一起

> with *prep.* 和……在一起
> be with 和……在一起
> together *adv.* 共同，一起，合起来，集拢地
> together with 和，加之

Mrs. Liu is _____ those children.

7. **family** *n.* 家庭（成员）

> family *n.* 家庭（成员）
> family circle 家庭圈子
> family corporation 家族公司
> family doctor 家庭医生

> family life　家庭生活
> family name　姓
> family tree　家谱，系谱图，族谱图

My _____ are all fond of the cinema.

8. **walk**　*v.* 走路，步行

> walk　*v.* 走路，步行
> walk around　绕……而走
> walk home　走回家
> walk into　走进
> walk over　走过

We _____ to school each day.

9. **over**　*prep.* 跨越，在……之上

> over　*prep.* 跨越，在……之上
> above　*prep.* 在……上方，胜过，超出
> top　*n.* 上部，顶部
> upper　*adj.* 上面的，上部的

The lamp hung _____ the table.

10. **bridge**　*n.* 桥

> bridge　*n.* 桥
> bridge table　桥牌桌
> bridge block　桥砖
> bridge cable　桥梁缆索

There is a _____ across the stream.

11. **boat**　*n.* 船

> boat　*n.* 船
> boat cover　船罩

boat race 赛船

ship *n.* 船，海船，舰

He is in his fishing _____ now.

12. **river** *n.* 河

river *n.* 河

riverside *n.* 河岸，河畔

riverbed *n.* 河床

riverbank *n.* 河堤

The longest _____ in Africa is the Nile.

13. **ship** *n.* 轮船

ship *n.* 轮船

ship carpenter 造船工人，造船木匠

ship construction 舰艇（船舶）建造

ship market 船舶市场

He has boarded a _____ for India.

14. **aeroplane** *n.* 飞机

aeroplane *n.* 飞机

airplane *n.* 飞机

plane *n.* 飞机（非正式用语）

aeroplane carrier 航空母舰

aeroplane oil 航空润滑油

aeroplane view 空（鸟）瞰图

aeroplanist *n.* 飞行家

The _____ is flying over the city.

15. **fly** *v.* 飞

fly *v.* 飞

fly ash 飞尘

> flying *adj.* 飞扬的，飞速的
> flying disk 飞碟

The plane will _____ from Paris to Rome.

Ⅱ Make sentences using the under-mentioned words 单词造句

sky — cloud

_____.

day — sun

_____.

sun — shine

_____.

with — family

_____.

walk — over

_____.

over — bridge

_____.

boat — river

_____.

river — ship

_____.

aeroplane — fly

_____.

Ⅲ Match 连线

- the upper atmosphere, seen as a hemisphere above   fly
  the earth
- a perceivable mass of watery vapor drifting in the   aeroplane
  sky

- time at which the sun is above the horizon   ship
- star which is the center of the solar system,   river
  providing the earth and other planets with heat and
  light
- make bright; glow   boat
- accompanied by or accompanying; together with   bridge
- a group of people come from the same blood; the   over
  member of the house
- to move on foot at a place slower than run   walk
- above; across   family
- structure connecting something or providing a path   with
  by joining two ends
- an object that can float on water and can transport   shine
  people
- large natural stream of water flowing into the sea,   sun
  lake or other stream
- large vessel sailing on the sea   day
- aircraft with wings   cloud
- move through the air with wings   sky

Ⅳ Glossary 词汇表

day   *n.* 日子
cloud *n.* 云
sky   *n.* 天空
sun   *n.* 太阳
shine *v.* 照耀
with   *prep.* 和……在一起

- family   *n.* 家庭（成员）
- walk   *v.* 走路，步行
- over   *prep.* 跨越，在……之上
- bridge   *n.* 桥
- boat   *n.* 船
- river   *n.* 河
- ship   *n.* 轮船
- aeroplane   *n.* 飞机
- fly   *v.* 飞

What are they doing?
他们在做什么？

I New words 新单词

1. **sleep** *v.* 睡觉

> sleep   *v.* 睡觉
> sleep late   睡过头，迟起
> sleep like a log   熟睡
> sleep like a top   酣睡
> sleeping   *n. & adj.* 睡眠；睡着的

I was so excited that I could hardly _____.

2. **shave** *v.* 刮脸

> shave   *v.* 刮脸
> shave off   剃去
> shaveling   *n.* 剃光头发的人，和尚，少年
> shaver   *n.* ［用具］剃须刀，修面的人

My father _____ every day.

3. **cry** *v.* 哭，喊

> cry   *v.* 哭，喊
> cry against   大声反对
> cry down   贬低，喝止
> cry for   吵着要，恳求，迫切需要

The boy _____ for help.

4. **wash** *v.* 洗

> wash *v.* 洗
>
> wash up 洗餐具
>
> wash-basin *n.* 洗脸盆
>
> wash away 洗掉，洗净，冲走，冲坏

He often helps his wife _____ the dishes.

5. **wait** *v.* 等

> wait *v.* 等
>
> wait and see 等着瞧
>
> wait for 等待
>
> wait out 等到……结束
>
> waiting *n. & adj.* 等待，服侍；等待的，服侍的

Don't _____ dinner for me.

6. **jump** *v.* 跳

> jump *v.* 跳
>
> jump over 跳过
>
> jump to 赶快，立即
>
> jump up 突然起立
>
> jumping *adj.* 跳跃的

They _____ off the wall and ran off.

Ⅱ *Make sentences using the under-mentioned words* 单词造句

sleep — wait

_____.

shave — wash

_____.

cry — jump

_____.

III Match 连线

- rest in a sleeping state
- to cut off hair with razor
- to give off sound or suffering, usually with tears
- to cleanse with water or other liquid
- to remain inactive in anticipation
- to push oneself into the air or away from a surface by the force of one's legs

jump
wait
wash
cry
shave
sleep

IV Glossary 词汇表

sleep   *v.* 睡觉
shave   *v.* 刮脸
cry   *v.* 哭，喊
wash   *v.* 洗
wait   *v.* 等
jump   *v.* 跳

Lesson
34 Our village
我们的村庄

I New words 新单词

1. **photograph** *n.* 照片

> photograph *n.* 照片
> photo *n.* 照片（非正式的）
> picture <美>照片
> take a photograph / picture of sb. 给某人拍照

I want to take a _____ .

2. **village** *n.* 村庄

> village *n.* 村庄
> villager *n.* 村民
> village community 村落社会，农村公社
> village fair trade 集市贸易
> country *n. & adj.* 国家，乡村，故乡；乡下的，
>   乡村的

We live in a small _____ .

3. **valley** *n.* 山谷

> valley *n.* 山谷
> valley floor 谷底
> valley side 峡谷边
> valley fog 谷雾

The trees and streams make the _____ very beautiful.

4. **between** *prep.* 在……之间

> between *prep.* 在……之间
> between A and B 在 A 与 B 之间
> between times 有时候，偶尔

The baby crawled _____ her father's legs.

5. **hill** *n.* 小山

> hill *n.* 小山
> mountain *n.* 山脉，山岳
> hill country 丘陵地
> hill features 山形，山地地貌
> hill people 山上的居民

I climbed up the _____ and ran down the other side.

6. **another** *adj.* 另外的

> another *adj.* 另外的
> other *adj.* 其他的，另外的，从前
> another place 另一个地方，另一议院
> another world 另外一个世界，来世（生）

This shirt is too big, and I'll try _____.

7. **wife** *n.* 妻子

> wife *n.* 妻子
> wifedom *n.* 妻的地位，为妻之道
> wifeless *adj.* 无妻的
> wifelike *adj.* 似妻的，适合做妻子的

She is a good _____ and mother.

8. **along** *prep.* 沿着

> along *prep.* 沿着
> down *prep.* 沿着，向下
> alongshore 沿着岸
> along with 连同……一起，随同……一起
> alongside *adv. & prep.* 在旁；横靠

The dogs are running _____ the river banks.

9. **bank** *n.* 河岸

> bank *n.* 河岸
> riverside *n.* 河岸

There are some big trees on the _____ of the river.

10. **water** *n.* 水

> water *n.* 水
> water-control *n.* 治水
> water bird 水鸟，水禽
> water body 水体，贮水池
> water bottle 水瓶，水袋，水壶

We can't live without _____.

11. **swim** *v.* 游泳

> swim *v.* 游泳
> go swimming 去游泳
> swim with the tide 随波逐流
> swimmer *n.* 游泳者
> swimming *n. & adj.* 游水，目眩；游泳（者）
>   的，游泳（者）用的，会游泳的

He can _____ two kilometer.

12. **building** *n.* 大楼，建筑物

> construction　*n.* 建筑，建筑物
> structure　*n.* 建筑，结构，建筑物
> building ground　建筑工地
> building industry　建筑工业

The new hospital is a big _____.

13. **park**　*n.* 公园

> park　*n.* 公园
> parkway　公园道路
> park nursery　公园苗圃
> garden　*n.* 花园

We are playing in the _____.

14. **into**　*prep.* 进入

> into　*prep.* 进入
> gointo　走进，进入
> look into　朝……里面看
> run into　偶遇，撞上
> turn into　把……变成……

They're going _____ the business world.

II Make sentences using the under-mentioned words 单词造句

photograph — village

_____.

valley — between

_____.

wife — park

_____.

building — into

_____.

hill — another

_____.

along — bank

_____.

water — swim

_____.

III Match 连线

- a picture obtained by using a camera and film sensitive to light   into
- collection of houses covering a small area than a town   park
- low land lying between hills and mountains   building
- in an area or interval separating two things or people   swim
- piece of land, usu. rounded, which is higher than its surrounding   water
- one more; additional   bank
- a woman to whom a man is married   along
- over; through   wife
- the land that is alongside a river   another
- the most common liquid, without color, taste or smell   hill
- travel through water by moving the body   between
- structure of a house-like thing   valley
- public recreation area with trees, meadow, etc.   village
- to the inside of   photograph

IV Glossary 词汇表

photograph　*n.* 照片

village　*n.* 村庄

valley　*n.* 山谷

between　*prep.* 在……之间

hill　*n.* 小山

another　*adj.* 另外的

wife　*n.* 妻子

along　*prep.* 沿

bank　*n.* 河岸

water　*n.* 水

swim　*v.* 游泳

building　*n.* 大楼，建筑物

park　*n.* 公园

into　*prep.* 进入

Lesson 35

Where...?

······在哪里？

1. **beside** *prep.* 在……旁

> beside *prep.* 在……旁
> alongside *adv.* 在旁，横靠
> by *adv.* 在附近，在旁边
> besides *prep. & adv.* 除……之外；此外

She sat down _____ her mother.

2. **off** *prep.* 离开

> off *prep.* 离开
> leave *v.* 动身，离开，出发
> take off 拿掉，取消，脱衣，起飞，减弱，离开
> off-key *adj.* 不平常的，走开的

Please take the curtains _____ their hooks.

II Make sentences using the under-mentioned words 单词造句

beside — off

_____ .

Ⅲ Match 连线

- at the side of   off
- away from or no longer in a place or position   beside

Ⅳ Glossary 词汇表

beside   *prep.* 在……旁
off   *prep.* 离开

Lesson 36

Making a bookcase

做书架

I New words 新单词

1. **work** *v.* 工作

> work *v.* 工作
> employment *n.* 工作，职业，雇佣
> job *n. & v.* 工作，零活
> labor *n.* 工作，劳动

We _____ five days a week.

2. **hard** *adv.* 努力地

> hard *adv.* 努力地
> struggle *n. & v.* 努力，奋斗；挣扎
> effort *n.* 努力，成就
> strive *v.* 努力，奋斗，斗争
> endeavor *n. & v.* 努力；尽力

They tried _____ to succeed.

3. **make** *v.* 做

> make *v.* 做
> do *v.* 做，实行
> make a bed 整理床铺
> make a choice 做一选择

He _____ a model plane out of wood.

4. **bookcase** *n.* 书橱，书架

> bookcase　*n.* 书橱，书架
> book　*n.* 书
> bookshop　*n.* 书店
> bookworm　*n.* 书虫，书呆子

There's a _____ near the blackboard.

5. **hammer** *n.* 锤子

> hammerhead　*n.* 锤头
> hammering　*n.* 锤打
> hammered　*adj.* 锤成的，铸打的
> hammer-harden　*n.* 锤炼

There is a _____ in the toolbox.

6. **paint** *v.* 上漆，涂

> paint　*v.* 上漆，涂
> scrawl　*v.* 乱涂，潦草的写
> paint box　颜料盒
> paint brush　漆刷
> paint drier　漆干剂

Who _____ this picture?

7. **pink** *n. & adj.* 粉红色；粉红色的

> pink　*n. & adj.* 粉红色；粉红色的
> in the pink　健康
> pink-collar　粉领的，职业妇女的
> pinklady　红粉佳人

I like those _____ flowers.

8. **favourite** *adj.* 最喜欢的

> favourite *adj.* 最喜欢的
> fond *adj.* 喜欢的，喜爱的
> like *adj.* 相似的，同样的
> love *v.* 爱，热爱

These novels are my _____.

II Make sentences using the under-mentioned words 单词造句

work — hard

_____.

make — favourite

_____.

hammer — bookcase

_____.

paint — pink

_____.

III Match 连线

- activity in which effort of the body or mind is used   favourite
  to produced something
- using great and steady effort   pink
- do; create   paint
- a piece of furniture containing shelves to hold   hammer
  books
- hand tool with a heavy metal head for driving nails   bookcase
  in
- to apply paint to a wall or door   make
- pale red color   hard

- beloved or preferred   work

Ⅳ Glossary 词汇表

work   *v.* 工作

hard   *adv.* 努力地

make   *v.* 做

bookcase   *n.* 书橱，书架

hammer   *n.* 锤子

paint   *v.* 上漆，涂

pink   *n. & adj.* 粉红色；粉红色的

favourite   *adj.* 最喜欢的

Lesson 37

What are you going to do? 你准备做什么?
What are you doing now? 你现在正在做什么?

I New words 新单词

1. **homework** *n.* 作业

> homework *n.* 作业
> do one's homework 做家庭作业
> exercise *n.* 练习，习题

Have you finished your _____?

2. **listen** *v.* 听

> listen *v.* 听（表示听的动作）
> listen to 听某人讲话
> hear *v.* 听说，听见，听到（表示听的结果）

You should _____ to the teacher if you want to learn.

3. **dish** *n.* 盘子，碟子

> dish *n.* 盘子，碟子
> dish up ［口］上菜，把……盛在盘中端上
> a homely dish 一道家常菜
> dishing *adj.* 碟形的
> plate *n.* 盘子，餐具

Mary puts the peaches in a white _____.

II Make sentences using the under-mentioned words 单词造句

homework — do

_____.

listen — speak

_____.

dish — dinner

_____.

III Match 连线

- work which a pupil is required to do at home after school
- try to hear something/somebody
- container for holding food

dish

listen

homework

IV Glossary 词汇表

homework   n. 作业
listen   v. 听
dish   n. 盘子，碟子

Lesson 38

Don't drop it!

别摔了！

I New words 新单词

1. **front**   *n.* 前面

> front   *n.* 前面
> front-line   *adj.* 前线的
> front and rear   在前后
> front door   前门
> front line   前排，前线
> front page news   头版新闻

The teacher called the boy to the _____.

2. **in front of**   在……之前

> in front of   在……之前
> in the front of   在……前部
> in front   在前面

There is a garden _____ the building.

3. **careful**   *adj.* 小心的，仔细的

> careful   *adj.* 小心的，仔细的
> carefully   *adv.* 小心地
> carefulness   *n.* 仔细，慎重
> careless   *adj.* 粗心的，疏忽的
> cautious   *adj.* 谨慎的，小心的

> Be careful! 小心点! (提醒他人可能发生的事故
>   或困难)

Lucy is a _____ girl.

4. **vase**   *n.* 花瓶

> vase   *n.* 花瓶
> flowerpot   *n.* 花盆
> vase painting   古希腊的瓶饰画，花瓶画

The problem is where we should put the _____.

5. **drop**   *v.* 掉下

> drop   *v.* 掉下
> drop-off   *n.* 急下降，直下降
> drop into   落入，偶然进入，不知不觉变得，训斥
> drop to   下降到，跌到

The plate _____ from her hands.

6. **flower**   *n.* 花

> flower   *n.* 花
> flower painting   花卉画
> flower pattern   花纹，花样
> flower show   花展
> flowerbed   *n.* 花床，花圃

The _____ are out.

Ⅱ *Make sentences using the under-mentioned words* 单词造句

front — drop

_____

in front of — careful

_____

vase — flower

_____.

Ⅲ Match 连线 . . . .

- the foremost part of anything   flower
- in the position directly before   drop
- doing something with a lot of care and concern   vase
- open container used as decoration or for holding   careful
  flowers
- fall or let fall in drops   in front of
- a plant which is conspicuous for its blossoms   front

Ⅳ Glossary 词汇表 . . . .

> front   *n.* 前面
>
> in front of   在……之前
>
> careful   *adj.* 小心的，仔细的
>
> vase   *n.* 花瓶
>
> drop   *v.* 掉下
>
> flower   *n.* 花

Lesson 39

What are you going to do? 你准备做什么？
I'm going to... 我准备……

1. **show** *v.* 给……看

> show *v.* 给……看
> show-off *n.* 卖弄，炫耀，虚饰
> show bill 海报，招贴
> show case 陈列柜，橱窗

He _____ me his pictures.

2. **send** *v.* 送给

> send *v.* 送给
> give *v.* 授予，给，捐献
> deliver *v.* 递送，给予
> send away 发送，派遣，驱逐，解雇

She _____ me a present.

3. **take** *v.* 带给

> take *v.* 带给
> bring *v.* 带来
> fetch *v.* 带来，取来

Please _____ him a cup of tea.

II Make sentences using the under-mentioned words 单词造句

show — take

_____.

send — letter

_____.

III Match 连线

- to offer for seeing   take
- to give out   send
- to move or carry from one place to another   show

IV Glossary 词汇表

show   v.   给……看
send   v.   送给
take   v.   带给

Lesson 40 Penny's bag
彭妮的提包

I New words 新单词

1. **cheese** *n.* 乳酪，干酪

> cheese *n.* 乳酪，干酪
> cream *n.* 乳酪，奶油
> cheese cake 干酪饼

She is baking a _____ cake.

2. **bread** *n.* 面包

> bread *n.* 面包
> bread and butter 涂黄油的面包
> bread and water 粗劣的饮食，粗茶淡饭
> bread and wine 圣餐
> bread baking 面包焙烤

Which would you like, _____ or noodles?

3. **soap** *n.* 肥皂

> soap *n.* 肥皂
> soap powder 肥皂粉
> soapbox *n.* 肥皂盒
> soap opera 肥皂剧
> soap bubble 肥皂泡

She washed her hands with _____.

4. **chocolate** *n.* 巧克力

> chocolate *n.* 巧克力
> chocolate bar 巧克力块（条）
> chocolate cake 巧克力大蛋糕
> chocolate mass 巧克力浆（糖料）
> chocolate pudding 巧克力布丁

I'd like a piece of _____.

5. **sugar** *n.* 糖

> sugar *n.* 糖
> candy *n.* 糖果，冰糖
> sugar bowl 糖罐
> sweet *n.* 糖果

_____ is under allocation during war time.

6. **coffee** *n.* 咖啡

> coffee *n.* 咖啡
> coffee cup 咖啡杯
> coffee bean 咖啡豆
> coffee house 咖啡厅

Would you like some _____?

7. **tea** *n.* 茶

> tea *n.* 茶
> green tea 绿茶
> black tea 红茶
> jasmine tea 花茶，茉莉花茶

I'd prefer a cup of _____.

8. **tobacco** *n.* 烟草，烟丝

> tobacco   *n.* 烟草，烟丝
> tobacconist   *n.* 烟草商
> smoke   *n.* 烟，烟尘

He gave up _____.

II Make sentences using the under-mentioned words 单词造句

cheese — bread

_____.

soap — clothes

_____.

chocolate — sugar

_____.

coffee — tea

_____.

tobacco — smoke

_____.

III Match 连线

- food produced from squeezed milk curds   tobacco
- a common food made of baked flour   tea
- substance used for cleaning things   coffee
- edible substance made from baked cocoa seeds   sugar
- sweet crystalline substance obtained from certain   chocolate
  kinds of care and beats
- a brown powder made by crushing the coffee beans   soap
  of tropical tree
- a hot brown drink made by pouring water onto   bread
  leaves of special kind

- group of plants the leaves of which are dried and   cheese
  prepared for smoking

IV Glossary 词汇表

cheese　*n.* 乳酪，干酪

bread　*n.* 面包

soap　*n.* 肥皂

chocolate　*n.* 巧克力

sugar　*n.* 糖

coffee　*n.* 咖啡

tea　*n.* 茶

tobacco　*n.* 烟草，烟丝

Is there a...in/on that...?

在那个……中 / 上有一个……吗？

Is there any...in/on that...?

在那个……中 / 上有……吗？

I New words 新单词

1. **bird** *n.* 鸟

> bird　*n.* 鸟
> bird's nest　鸟巢
> bird's eye　鸟瞰的
> birdseed　鸟饵

A _____ in the hand is worth two in the bush.

2. **any** *adv.* 一些

> any　*adv.* 一些
> some　*adv.* 一些，若干
> several　*adj.* 几个的，个别的
> few　*adj.* 一些，少数的
> little　*adj.* 少许，很少的

I didn't eat _____ meat.

3. **some** *adv.* 一些

> some   *adv.* 一些
> some time ago   不久前
> some other time   改天吧
> some few   有一些，不少，颇有几个

There is _____ ice in the fridge.

II Make sentences using the under-mentioned words 单词造句

bird — some

_____ .

any — people

_____ .

III Match 连线

- feathered animal with wings which enable them to fly   some
- any or a few more than three   bird
- not a particular quantity or number of   any

IV Glossary 词汇表

> bird   *n.* 鸟
> any   *adv.* 一些
> some   *adv.* 一些

42

Hurry up!

快点!

I New words 新单词

· ·

1. **of course** 当然

> of course 当然
>
> certainly 当然
>
> sure 当然

That was 40 years ago, but _____ you wouldn't remember it.

2. **kettle** *n.* 水壶

> kettle *n.* 水壶
>
> canteen *n.* （军用的）水壶
>
> jug *n.* 水壶，监牢

Please boil the _____ and make some tea.

3. **behind** *prep.* 在……后面

> behind *prep.* 在……后面
>
> behind schedule 落后于预定计划
>
> behind the curtain 幕后，秘密
>
> behind time 迟了

The train was _____ time.

4. **teapot** *n.* 茶壶

teapot   *n.* 茶壶
tea party   茶话会
tea table   茶几

It is about letting people know that you have a hundred dollars to spend on a _____.

5. **now**   *adv.* 现在，此刻

now   *adv.* 现在，此刻
now and again   不时
now and then   偶尔
now that   既然

Shall we go _____?

6. **find**   *v.* 找到

find   *v.* 找到，强调结果
look for   表示寻找的动作，不强调结果
seek   *v.* 寻找

Shall we ever _____ an answer to the tough problem?

7. **boil**   *v.* 沸腾，开

boil   *v.* 沸腾，开
boil dry   煮干，蒸发至干
boil away   不断沸腾，汽化
boiled   煮沸的，煮熟的

When water _____ it changes into steam.

Ⅱ *Make sentences using the under-mentioned words* 单词造句

of course — now

_____.

kettle — boil

_____.

behind — find

_____.

teapot — water

_____.

Ⅲ Match 连线

- sure; certainly
- metal container with a spout and handle, for boiling water in
- at the back of
- a container with a handle and spout, in which tea is made and served
- at present
- look for; search
- use fire to heat

boil
find

now
teapot

behind
kettle
of course

Ⅳ Glossary 词汇表

of course 当然
kettle *n.* 水壶
behind *prep.* 在……后面
teapot *n.* 茶壶
now *adv.* 现在，此刻
find *v.* 找到
boil *v.* 沸腾，开

Lesson
43

The boss's letter
老板的信

I New words 新单词 ....

1. **can** *v.* 能够

can	*v.* 能够
can not	不能
able	*adj.* 能够的，能干的，能力
capable	*adj.* 有能力的，能干的

   She _____ drive now.

2. **boss** *n.* 老板，上司

boss	*n.* 老板，上司
employer	*n.* 雇主，老板
manager	*n.* 经理，管理人员，管理器

   She asks her _____ for a pay rise.

3. **minute** *n.* 分（钟）

minute	*n.* 分（钟）
second	*n.* 秒（钟）
a minute/ one minute	一分钟，一会儿

   Please wait a _____.

4. **ask** *v.* 请求，要求

ask   *v.* 请求，要求
ask for   请求，寻找
ask about   问（某人）关于某事
request   *v.* 请求，要求

May I _____ a favour of you？

5. **handwriting**   *n.* 书写

handwriting   *n.* 书写
handwriting reader   手写体阅读机
handwrite   *v.* 用手写，亲手写
handwritten   *adj.* 手写的

I can't read his _____.

6. **terrible**   *adj.* 糟糕的，可怕的

terrible   *adj.* 糟糕的，可怕的
awful   *adj.* 糟糕的，可怕的，极度的
terribly   *adv.* 可怕地，十分，极

She is _____ at maths.

II *Make sentences using the under-mentioned words 单词造句*

can — boss

_____.

minute — ask

_____.

handwriting — terrible

_____.

III Match 连线

- able to   terrible
- head or principal; controller or master   handwriting
- sixtieth of an hour   ask
- request   minute
- writing by hand with writing utensils   boss
- causing terror or fear; dreadful   can

IV Glossary 词汇表

can   *v.* 能够
boss   *n.* 老板，上司
minute *n.* 分（钟）
ask   *v.* 请求，要求
handwriting   *n.* 书写
terrible   *adj.* 糟糕的，可怕的

Lesson 44

Can you...?
你能……吗？

I New words 新单词

1. **lift** *v.* 拿起，搬起，举起

> lift *v.* 拿起，搬起，举起
> take up 拿起
> raise *v.* 举起，增加

The elderly lady _____ her eyes from the book.

2. **cake** *n.* 饼，蛋糕

> cake *n.* 饼，蛋糕
> snack *n.* 点心，小吃
> cake flour 细面粉
> cake product 糕点

What about another _____ ?

3. **biscuit** *n.* 饼干

> biscuit *n.* 饼干
> cookies *n.* 饼干
> biscuit bakery 饼干烘房
> biscuit dough 饼干面团

These _____ you baked are delicious.

II Make sentences using the under-mentioned words 单词造句

lift — box

_____.

cake — biscuit

_____.

III Match 连线

- raise; take up   cake
- food that is made by baking th emixture of flour,   biscuit
  sugar, butter, etc.
- a small, thin, unleavened dough which is baked   lift
  crisp and eaten

IV Glossary 词汇表

lift   *v.* 拿起，搬起，举起

cake   *n.* 饼，蛋糕

biscuit   *n.* 饼干

Lesson 45

A cup of coffee
一杯咖啡

I New words 新单词

1. **like** *v.* 喜欢，想要

> like *v.* 喜欢，想要
> love *v.* 爱，热爱，爱慕
> likely *adj. & adv.* 很可能的，有希望的；或许，很可能
> likeness *n.* 相像，相似物
> liken *v.* 把……比作

On Sundays I _____ to sleep late.

2. **want** *v.* 想

> want *v.* 想
> desire *v.* 想要，期望
> want for 缺少，缺乏，需要
> want sb. to do sth. 想某人做某事

I _____ a bicycle for my birthday.

II Make sentences using the under-mentioned words 单词造句

like — flower

_____.

want — job

- enjoy; find pleasant   like
- to wish for; desire   want

like   *v.* 喜欢，想要
want   *v.* 想

Lesson 46

Do you like...?
你喜欢……吗？

Do you want...?
你想要……吗？

I New words 新单词

1. **fresh** *adj.* 新鲜的

> fresh   *adj.* 新鲜的
> fresh air   新鲜空气
> fresh blood   新成员
> fresh fruit   鲜果
> green   *adj.* 绿色的，未成熟的，新鲜的

The air smelt _____ after the rain.

2. **egg** *n.* 鸡蛋

> egg   *n.* 鸡蛋
> egg-shaped   *adj.* 蛋形的
> egg-spoon   *n.* 吃煮蛋的小匙，蛋匙
> egg-white   *n.* 蛋白，蛋清
> eggshell   *n.* 蛋壳
> yolk   *n.* 蛋黄

We have boiled _____ for breakfast every day.

3. **butter** *n.* 黄油

butter	*n.* 黄油
butter cake	奶油蛋糕
butter maker	奶油制造者
butter bread	涂奶油面包片，奶油面包

Shall I use oil or _____ for frying the onions?

4. **pure** *adj.* 纯净的

pure	*adj.* 纯净的
purify	*v.* 净化
purity	*n.* 纯净，纯度
pureness	*n.* 纯粹，干净

The water in Mountain Rivers is usually _____.

5. **honey** *n.* 蜂蜜

honey	*n.* 蜂蜜
honey bee	蜜蜂
honey aroma	蜜香
honey comb	蜂巢
honey peach	水蜜桃

Would you like some _____?

6. **ripe** *adj.* 成熟的

ripe	*adj.* 成熟的
ripeness	*n.* 成熟，老练
mature	*adj. &v.* 成熟（的），到期（的）
adult	*adj.* 成人的，成熟的

This fruit isn't _____ yet.

7. **banana** *n.* 香蕉

banana　*n.* 香蕉

banana pin　香蕉（形）插头

banana oil　＜美俚＞说大话，假话，空话，胡说八道

I'd like some _____ .

8. **jam**　*n.* 果酱

jam　*n.* 果酱

jam-jar　*n.* 果酱罐

jam filler　果酱装填机

She takes out a jar of _____ and gives to me.

9. **sweet**　*adj.* 甜的

sweet　*adj.* 甜的

sweetening　*n.* 甜的调味料

sweetie　*n.* 甜的糕饼类

sweetly　*adv.* 甜美地

I don't like _____ coffee.

10. **orange**　*n.* 橙

orange　*n.* 橙

orange blossom　橙花

orange juice　橘子汁

orange meal　橘皮粉

Do you like _____ ?

11. **Scotch whisky**　苏格兰威士忌

Scotch whisky　苏格兰威士忌

Scotch carpet　苏格兰地毯

Scotch egg　苏格兰煮蛋

His father likes _____ very much.

12. **choice** *adj.* 上等的，精选的

> choice   *adj.* 上等的，精选的
> choice beef   精选级牛肉
> choice goods   精选品，上等品
> choice grade   精选级

The _____ of the enemy troops has been completely wiped out.

13. **apple** *n.* 苹果

> apple   *n.* 苹果
> apple-pie   *n.* 苹果饼（俗称苹果派）
> apple brandy   苹果白兰地
> apple butter   苹果酱
> apple green   苹果绿

She is eating an apple _____.

14. **wine** *n.* 酒，果酒

> wine   *n.* 酒，果酒
> wine-colored   *adj.* 深红色的
> wine-cup   *n.* 葡萄酒杯
> wine bar   酒吧，小酒馆

Drinking one glass of red _____ every day may have certain health benefits.

15. **beer** *n.* 啤酒

> beer   *n.* 啤酒
> beer-cellar   *n.* 啤酒窖
> beer-mat   *n.* 啤酒杯垫
> beer bottle   啤酒瓶

Most _____ are made from barley.

16. **blackboard** *n.* 黑板

> blackboard   *n.* 黑板
>
> blackboard paint   黑板漆
>
> scrubbing brush   板刷
>
> chalk   *n.* 粉笔

Please look at the _____ !

II *Make sentences using the under-mentioned words* 单词造句

fresh — egg

_____.

butter — bread

_____.

pure — beer

_____.

honey — sweet

_____.

ripe — banana

_____.

jam — orange

_____.

scotch whisky — choice

_____.

apple — wine

_____.

blackboard — write

_____.

III *Match* 连线

• newly made or produced   blackboard

- hard-shelled oval body produced by the female of birds and other animal — beer
- fairly solid yellow fat made from milk or cream and spread on bread — wine
- not mixed with any other substance — apple
- sweet, thick substance made by bees from the nectar of flowers — choice
- fully developed; mature — Scotch whisky
- crescent-shaped fruit — orange
- very thick sweet liquid made from fruit boiled and preserved in sugar, used esp. for spreading on bread — sweet
- tasting as if it contains sugar — jam
- reddish-yellow — banana
- a strong alcoholic drink made in Scotland — ripe
- high quality — honey
- a hard round fruit with white juicy and a red, green, or yellow skin — pure
- an alcoholic drink made from grapes — butter
- an alcoholic drink made from malt and made bitter with hops — egg
- a dark smooth surface used esp. in schools for writing or drawing on, usu. with chalk — fresh

IV Glossary 词汇表

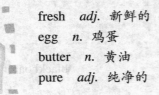

fresh   *adj.* 新鲜的
egg   *n.* 鸡蛋
butter   *n.* 黄油
pure   *adj.* 纯净的

honey   n. 蜂蜜

ripe   adj. 成熟的

banana   n. 香蕉

jam   n. 果酱

sweet   adj. 甜的

orange   n. 橙

Scotch whisky   苏格兰威士忌

choice   adj. 上等的，精选的

apple   n. 苹果

wine   n. 酒，果酒

beer   n. 啤酒

blackboard   n. 黑板

Lesson 47

At the butcher's
在肉店

1. butcher *n.* 卖肉者

> butcher   *n.* 卖肉者
> butcher cow   肉用牛，菜牛
> butcher knife   屠刀
> butchery   *n.* 屠场，肉贩
> the butcher's   肉店

If you want to buy the freshest meat, you should go to the _____.

2. meat *n.* （食用）肉

> meat   *n.* （食用）肉
> meat-eating   *adj.* 食肉的
> meat and drink   饭食，乐趣
> meat dumpling   肉汤团，肉馅水饺

We always cook _____.

3. beef *n.* 牛肉

> beef   *n.* 牛肉
> fork   *n.* 猪肉
> mutton   *n.* 羊肉

· 174 ·

beef ham　牛腿肉，无骨牛臀肉
beef jerky　牛肉干

He loves _____ steak.

4. **lamb**　*n.* 羔羊肉

lamb　*n.* 羔羊肉
lamb splitter　剔羊排刀，羊肉分割机
lamb tail　羔羊尾藤
sheep　*n.* 羊，绵羊

I'd prefer _____ chops.

5. **husband**　*n.* 丈夫

husband　*n.* 丈夫
husband like　丈夫似的
man　*n.* 人类，男人，丈夫
wife　*n.* 妻子

He will make an ideal _____ for you.

6. **steak**　*n.* 牛排

steak　*n.* 牛排
steak-house　*n.* 牛排餐厅
steak piece　＜英＞牛后腰肉，肋骨肉

We'll have beef _____ for dinner.

7. **mince**　*n.* 肉馅

mince　*n.* 肉馅
mince pie　肉馅饼
mince meat　肉馅子，肉末
minced chicken　鸡肉酱

He is stuffed with _____ pies.

8. **chicken** *n.* 鸡

> chicken   *n.* 鸡
> chicken house   鸡场
> chicken salad   鸡丁沙拉
> chicken sticks   鸡肉条（冷冻半成品）
> chicken broth   鸡汤

This chicken is ＿＿＿＿＿＿＿.

9. **tell** *v.* 告诉

> tell   *v.* 告诉
> to tell you the truth   老实说，说实话
> to tell the truth   老实说，说实话
> tell a lie   说谎，撒谎
> tell of   讲述

Please ＿＿＿＿＿＿＿ me what happened.

10. **truth** *n.* 实情

> truth   *n.* 实情
> truthful   *adj.* 诚实的，说实话的
> truthfulness   *n.* 真实，正当，坦率
> fact   *n.* 事实，事情，实际

There is no ＿＿＿＿＿＿＿ in what he says.

11. **either** *adv.* 也

> either   *adv.* 也
> too   *adv.* 也（用于否定句），常用于肯定句，
>   有时也用于疑问句，但不能用于否定句。常见
>   于句末，too 前常有逗号
> also   *adv.* 也，同样（可用于句首，句中）

If you don't go, I won't ＿＿＿＿＿＿＿.

Ⅱ Make sentences using the under-mentioned words 单词造句

butcher — meat

_____ .

beef — steak

_____ .

lamb — either

_____ .

husband — man

_____ .

mince — chicken

_____ .

tell — truth

_____ .

Ⅲ Match 连线

- one who kills animals and sells their meat for food   either
- flesh of animals used for food, excluding fish   truth
- mature steer, bull, ox, or cow which can be eaten   tell
- the flesh of young sheep   chicken
- a married man   mince
- Slice of meat or fish for cooking   steak
- minced meat   husband
- a common farmyard bird; common young domestic   lamb
  poultry
- express with words; narrate; inform   beef
- something that is true, or conforms to reality   meat
- likewise; also   butcher

IV Glossary 词汇表

butcher   *n.* 卖肉者

meat   *n.*（食用）肉

beef   *n.* 牛肉

lamb   *n.* 羔羊肉

husband   *n.* 丈夫

steak   *n.* 牛排

mince   *n.* 肉馅

chicken   *n.* 鸡

tell   *v.* 告诉

truth   *n.* 实情

either   *adv.* 也

Lesson 48

He likes...
他喜欢……
But he doesn't like...
但是他不喜欢……

I New words 新单词

1. **tomato** *n.* 西红柿

   > tomato   *n.* 西红柿
   > tomato bread   番茄面包
   > tomato ketchup/paste   番茄酱
   > tomato salad   番茄色拉

   _____ can be eaten raw.

2. **potato** *n.* 土豆

   > potato   *n.* 土豆
   > potato crisp   （BrE.）炸薯条
   > potato chip   炸土豆片
   > potato peeler   马铃薯（土豆）去皮机

   _____ grows in many parts of the world.

3. **cabbage** *n.* 卷心菜

   > cabbage   *n.* 卷心菜
   > cabbage mustard   芥蓝
   > cabbage shredder   卷心菜切丝机

   _____ is a member of the vegetable kingdom.

4. **lettuce** *n.* 莴苣

> lettuce *n.* 莴苣
> cabbage lettuce 结球莴苣，卷心莴苣

Go and buy a couple of _____.

5. **pea** *n.* 豌豆

> pea *n.* 豌豆
> pea bean 菜豆
> pea green 淡绿色，青豆色
> pea shell 豌豆荚
> pea soup 豌豆汤

This _____ soup is very delicious.

6. **bean** *n.* 豆角

> bean *n.* 豆角
> bean-pod *n.* 豆荚
> bean cake 豆糟，豆饼
> bean curd 豆腐
> bean milk 豆浆

Which do you prefer, _____ milk or milk?

7. **pear** *n.* 梨

> pear *n.* 梨
> pear drop 梨形糖果
> pear nectar （带肉）梨汁饮料

The _____ is rotten to the core.

8. **grape** *n.* 葡萄

> grape *n.* 葡萄
> grapery *n.* 葡萄园

grape vine 葡萄藤
grape sugar 葡萄糖
grape-brandy *n.* 葡萄白兰地酒
grape ice 冰冻葡萄汁

Wine is made from _____.

9. **peach** *n.* 桃

peach *n.* 桃
peach-colored *adj.* 桃色的
peach blossom 桃花

The little girl likes tinned _____.

Ⅱ Make sentences using the under-mentioned words 单词造句

tomato — potato

_____.

cabbage — lettuce

_____.

pea — bean

_____.

pear — peach

_____.

grape — sour

_____.

Ⅲ Match 连线

• vegetable widely grown in many places which is   peach
fleshy, red, smooth-skinned

- a round root vegetable with a thin brown or yellowish skin
grape
- vegetable with overlapping leaves around the head with a thick root
pear
- a round vegetable with thin pale green leaves, used raw in salads
lettuce
- highly nourishing seeds in pods
bean
- seeds of any of various upright climbing plants, esp. one that can be eat
cabbage
- a sweet juicy fruit, which has a round base and usu. becomes narrower towards the stem
pea
- edible fruit growing in bunches on vines, from which wine can be made
potato
- round juicy fruit with delicate yellowish-red skin and a stone-like seed
tomato

IV Glossary 词汇表

tomato　*n.* 西红柿

potato　*n.* 土豆

cabbage　*n.* 卷心菜

lettuce　*n.* 莴苣

pea　*n.* 豌豆

bean　*n.* 豆角

pear　*n.* 梨

grape　*n.* 葡萄

peach　*n.* 桃

A pleasant climate
宜人的气候

I New words 新单词

1. **Greece** *n.* 希腊

> Greece *n.* 希腊
> Greek *n.* 希腊人，希腊语；*adj.* 希腊的，希腊人的

_____ is a country of southeast Europe.

2. **climate** *n.* 气候

> climate *n.* 气候（指某一地区数年间的天气情况）
> What's the climate like...? 气候怎么样？
> Weather *n.* 天气，气象，气候

She is not used to living in a cold _____.

3. **country** *n.* 国家

> country *n.* 国家
> nation *n.* 国家，民族
> state *n.* 国家，政府，州

India and Thailand are Asian _____.

4. **pleasant** *adj.* 宜人的

> pleasant   *adj.* 宜人的
> delightful   *adj.* 愉快的，可喜的
> pleasance   *n.* 快乐，游乐园
> pleasant note   愉快香韵

This study is _____ to work in.

5. **weather**   *n.* 天气

> weather   *n.* 天气
> Weather forecast   天气预报

The _____ gradually fined after a heavy shower.

6. **spring**   *n.* 春季

> spring   *n.* 春季
> spring barley   春（播）大麦
> in spring   在春季
> spring begins   立春（中国农历二十四节气之一）

In _____ leaves begin to grow on the trees.

7. **windy**   *adj.* 有风的

> windy   *adj.* 有风的
> wind   *n.* 风

The winter here is cold, dry, and _____.

8. **warm**   *adj.* 温暖的

> warm   *adj.* 温暖的
> warm-blooded   *adj.* 热血的，热烈的
> warm-hearted   *adj.* 热诚的，热心的
> warm-up   *n.* 准备动作，热身

It is _____ today.

9. **rain**　*v.* 下雨

> rain　*v.* 下雨
> rain-belt　*n.* 多雨地带，雨带
> rain forest　（热带的）雨林
> rainbow　*n.* 彩虹
> rainy　*adj.* 下雨的，多雨的

It ＿＿＿＿＿＿＿ last night.

10. **sometimes**　*adv.* 有时

> sometimes　*adv.* 有时
> some times　一些次数
> sometime　某时
> some time　一些时间

＿＿＿＿＿＿＿ she helps her mother in the house.

11. **summer**　*n.* 夏天

> summer　*n.* 夏天
> summer-house　*n.* 凉亭
> summer vocation　暑期
> summer camp　*n.* 夏令营

Where have you spent your ＿＿＿＿＿＿＿ holiday?

12. **autumn**　*n.* 秋天

> autumn　*n.* ＜英＞秋天
> fall　*n.* ＜美＞秋天
> autumn begins　立秋
> autumn seeding　秋播

It has been one of the coldest ＿＿＿＿＿＿＿ for years.

13. **winter**　*n.* 冬天

> winter   *n.* 冬天
> winter crop   冬播作物
> winter drying   冬季干旱
> winter sleep   冬眠
> winter solstice   冬至

We have passed the last few _____ in the south.

14. **snow**   *v.* 下雪

> snow   *v.* 下雪
> snow-white   *adj.* 雪白的，纯白的
> snow cover   积雪（层），雪盖
> snow melt   融雪

It has been _____ for 3 days here.

15. **January**   *n.* 1 月

> January   *n.* 1 月
> Jan.   *n.* 1 月，January 的缩写

He was born on 3 _____.

16. **February**   *n.* 2 月

> February   *n.* 2 月
> Feb.   *n.* 2 月，February 的缩写

_____ is the second month of the year.

17. **March**   *n.* 3 月

> March   *n.* 3 月
> Mar.   *n.* 3 月，March 的缩写

Today is 20th, _____.

18. **April**   *n.* 4 月

April　*n.* 4 月

Apr.　*n.* 4 月，April 的缩写

April fool　愚人节中受愚弄者，愚弄的行为

April Fools' Day　愚人节

April fish　［谑］愚人节的受愚弄者

The weather is usually changeable in _____.

19. **May**　*n.* 5 月

May　*n.* 5 月

May Day　国际劳动节

May queen　5 月皇后（May Day 所选出的美女）

They'll go on holiday in _____.

20. **June**　*n.* 6 月

June　*n.* 6 月

Jun.　*n.* 6 月，June 的缩写

June Solstice　［天］夏至

Children's Day is on 1 _____.

21. **July**　*n.* 7 月

July　*n.* 7 月

Jul.　*n.* 7 月，July 的缩写

_____ comes after June.

22. **August**　*n.* 8 月

August　*n.* 8 月

Aug.　*n.* 8 月，August 的缩写

Our contract will run out in _____.

23. **September**　*n.* 9 月

> September *n.* 9 月
> Sep. *n.* 9 月，September 的缩写

The first term begins in _____.

24. **October** *n.* 10 月

> October *n.* 10 月
> Oct. *n.* 10 月，October 的缩写

She will be 24 in _____.

25. **November** *n.* 11 月

> November *n.* 11 月
> Nov. *n.* 11 月，November 的缩写

He will arrive on 5 _____.

26. **December** *n.* 12 月

> December *n.* 12 月
> Dec. *n.* 12 月，December 的缩写
> December Solstice ［天］冬至

_____ is the last month of the year.

Ⅱ *Make sentences using the under-mentioned words* 单词造句

greece — country

_____.

climate — pleasant

_____.

weather — spring

_____.

January — cold

_____.

February — windy

March — warm

_____.

April — rain

_____.

May — sometimes

_____.

June — summer

_____.

July — hot

_____.

August — autumn

_____.

September — student

_____.

October — cool

_____.

November — winter

_____.

December — snow

_____.

III Match 连线

- a European country whose capital is Athens
- the regular weather condition of an area
- a nation or state
- pleasing; agreeable
- state of atmospheric conditions, e. g. , sunshine, rain, wind, etc.
- the first season of a year

December
November
October
September
August

July

- a lot of wind
- moderately hot
- water falling in separate drops from the clouds
- on some occasions
- the warmest season of the year
- the third season of a year
- coldest season of the year
- ice crystal that is formed from water-condensed vapor in the air
- the first month of the year
- the second month of the year
- the third month of the year
- the fourth month of the year
- the fifth month of the year
- the sixth month of the year
- the seventh month of the year
- the eighth month of the year
- the ninth month of the year
- the tenth month of the year
- the eleventh month of the year
- the twelfth month of the year

June
May
April
March
February
January
snow
winter

autumn
summer
sometimes
rain
warm
windy
spring
weather
pleasant
country
climate
Greece

IV Glossary 词汇表

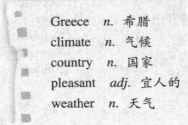

Greece   *n.* 希腊
climate   *n.* 气候
country   *n.* 国家
pleasant *adj.* 宜人的
weather   *n.* 天气

spring   *n.* 春季

windy   *adj.* 有风的

warm   *adj.* 温暖的

rain   *v.* 下雨

sometimes   *adv.* 有时

summer   *n.* 夏天

autumn   *n.* 秋天

winter   *n.* 冬天

snow   *v.* 下雪

January   *n.* 1 月

February   *n.* 2 月

March   *n.* 3 月

April   *n.* 4 月

May   *n.* 5 月

June   *n.* 6 月

July   *n.* 7 月

August   *n.* 8 月

September   *n.* 9 月

October   *n.* 10 月

November   *n.* 11 月

December   *n.* 12 月

Lesson 50

What nationality are they?
他们是哪国人？
Where do they come from?
他们来自哪个国家？

I New words 新单词

1. **the U. S.** 美国

> the U. S.　美国
> the United States of America　*n.* 美国，其缩写为
> 　　the U. S. A.　或 the U. S.
> America　*n.* 美国

He has already been in _____ .

2. **Brazil** *n.* 巴西

> Brazil　*n.* 巴西
> Brazil coffee　巴西咖啡
> Brazilian　*n. & adj.* 巴西人；巴西的

_____ is a beautiful country.

3. **Holland** *n.* 荷兰

> Holland　*n.* 荷兰
> Dutch　*n. & adj.* 荷兰人，荷兰语；荷兰的

The chairman is in _____ on business.

4. **England** *n.* 英国

> England *n.* 英国
> English *n. & adj.* 英国人，英语；英文的
> British *adj.* 英国的
> Britain *n.* 英国

There are many ports in _____.

5. **France** *n.* 法国

> France *n.* 法国
> French *n. & adj.* 法语；法国的，法国人的
> French bean 法国菜豆

Paris is the capital of _____.

6. **Germany** *n.* 德国

> Germany *n.* 德国
> German *n. & adj.* 德语；德国的，德国人的

_____ was unified in 1871.

7. **Italy** *n.* 意大利

> Italy *n.* 意大利
> Italian *n. & adj.* 意大利语；意大利的，意大利人的

_____ is a peninsula.

8. **Norway** *n.* 挪威

> Norway *n.* 挪威
> Norwegian *n. & adj.* 挪威语；挪威的，挪威人的

He is a native of _____.

9. **Russia** *n.* 俄罗斯

> Russia *n.* 俄罗斯
> Russian *n. & adj.* 俄语；俄罗斯的，俄罗斯人的

Have you ever been to _____?

10. **Spain** *n.* 西班牙

> Spain *n.* 西班牙
> Spanish *n. & adj.* 西班牙语；西班牙的，西班牙人的

They arrive in _____ yesterday.

11. **Sweden** *n.* 瑞典

> Sweden *n.* 瑞典
> Swedish *n. & adj.* 瑞典语；瑞典的，瑞典人的

They migrated eastward to _____.

Ⅱ *Make sentences using the under-mentioned words* 单词造句

The U. S. — Brazil

_____.

Holland — Italy

_____.

England — Spain

_____.

France — Germany

_____.

Norway — Sweden

_____.

Russia — country

_____.

Ⅲ Match 连线

• a Northern European country whose capital is stockholm   Brazil

- a country in South America whose capital is Brasilia   Sweden
- largest country in Asia which spans Eastern Europe   Holland
  and Northern Asia
- a country in Northern Europe whose capital is Oslo   England
- a European country whose capital is Rome   France
- one of the countries in Europe whose capital is Paris   Germany
- a country in the United Kingdom   Norway
- a country in Europe whose capital is Amsterdam   Russia

IV Glossary 词汇表

the U. S.   美国

Brazil   *n.* 巴西

Holland   *n.* 荷兰

England   *n.* 英国

France   *n.* 法国

Germany   *n.* 德国

Italy   *n.* 意大利

Norway   *n.* 挪威

Russia   *n.* 俄罗斯

Spain   *n.* 西班牙

Sweden   *n.* 瑞典

51 An interesting climate
有趣的气候

Ⅰ New words 新单词

1. **mild** *adj.* 温和的，温暖的

> mild *adj.* 温和的，温暖的
> gentle *adj.* 温和的，文雅的
> warm *adj.* 温暖的，暖和的

John is a _____ man who never raises his voice.

2. **always** *adv.* 总是

> always *adv.* 总是
> at all time 总是
> always on top 总在最上面

He _____ comes late.

3. **north** *n.* 北方

> north *n.* 北方
> North-East *n.* 东北
> North-West *n.* 西北
> North America 北美洲

The _____ central states have a very different kind of climate.

4. **east** *n.* 东方

east   *n.* 东方

East End   （英国）伦敦东区，东伦敦

East coast fever   海岸热

The sun rises in the _____.

5. **wet**   *adj.* 潮湿的

wet   *adj.* 潮湿的

wet air pump   湿气泵

wet body   湿体

wet climate   常湿气候

wet cleaner   湿式除尘器；煤气洗涤器，湿法洗涤器

The grass is _____ with dew.

6. **west**   *n.* 西方

west   *n.* 西方

west end   伦敦西区

westbound   *adj.* 向西进行的，西行的

westbound train   西行列车

The rain is coming from the _____.

7. **south**   *n.* 南方

south   *n.* 南方

south-eastern   *adj.* 东南的；位于东南方的（国家）

south-polar   *adj.* 南极的

South Africa   南非（非洲南部的一个国家）

There is a strong _____ wind today.

8. **season**   *n.* 季节

season   *n.* 季节

seasonal   *adj.* 季节的，季节性的，周期性的

season ticket   季票，长期票

_____ is the hottest season here.

9. **best** *adv.* 最

> best *adv.* 最
> best author 畅销书作者
> best-selling *adj.* 最畅销的，最红的
> best of all 最好的

We had _____ call for the doctor at once.

10. **night** *n.* 夜晚

> night *n.* 夜晚
> night school 夜校
> night and day 夜以继日
> evening *n.* 傍晚，晚上

She works _____.

11. **rise** *v.* 升起

> rise *v.* 升起
> rising *adj.* 上升的，上涨的；*n.* 上升，起立，
>   起义
> uprising *n.* 升起，起义
> risen rise 的过去分词；*adj.* 升起的
> raise *v.* 升起，提高，饲养，筹集，使复活

The level of the river is still _____.

12. **early** *adv.* 早

> early *adv.* 早
> early and late 从早到晚
> early or late 迟早
> early bird 早起者，早到者

The secretary always arrives _____.

13. **set**　*v.*（太阳）落下去

> set　*v.*（太阳）落下去
> fall　*v.* 落下，下跌
> drop　*v.* 滴下，落下
> downfall　*n.* 落下，衰败，垮台

The moon is _____.

14. **late**　*adv.* 晚，迟

> late　*adv.* 晚，迟
> lately　*adv.* 近来，最近
> late-night　*adj.* 深夜的，午夜的
> late frost　晚霜
> late shift　夜班
> late start　出发过迟

I was _____ for school this morning.

15. **interesting**　*adj.* 有趣的，有意思的

> interesting　*adj.* 有趣的，有意思的
> interestingly　*adv.* 有趣地
> interested　*adj.* 感兴趣的，有成见的，有权益的
> funny　*adj.* 有趣的，奇怪的，滑稽的
> amusing　*adj.* 有趣的

Is the story _____?

16. **subject**　*n.* 话题

> subject　*n.* 话题
> subject fields　主题领域
> subject matter　主题，主旨

> topic   *n.* 话题，主题，论题
> theme   *n.* 主题，题目

I was the _____ of their talk.

17. **conversation**   *n.* 谈话

> conversation   *n.* 谈话
> talk   *n. & v.* 谈话，议论，演讲
> speech   *n.* 演说，讲话
> speak   *v.* 讲话，谈话

I had a long _____ with your teacher.

Ⅱ Make sentences using the under-mentioned words 单词造句

subject — conversation

_____.

late — always

_____.

east — rise

_____.

north — night

_____.

mild — season

_____.

interesting — best

_____.

set — west

_____.

early — south

_____.

Ⅲ Match 连线

- gentle; moderate in intensity, not too harsh or too drastic
- continuously; on every occasion
- the direction where the sun comes up in the morning
- the direction that is on your left when you watch the sun come up in the morning
- after the usual or right time
- before the usual or right time
- something you are talking or writing about
- arousing interest
- talk; speech
- the action that the sun goes down from the sky
- the part of the day between the afternoon and when you do to bed
- not dry
- go up
- most good
- where the sun goes down in the evening
- one of the four parts of the year
- the direction that is on your right when you watch the sun come up in the morning

late

east

north

always

mild

subject

interesting

conversation

set

early

rise

night

wet

season

south

west

best

Ⅳ Glossary 词汇表

mild   *adj.* 温和的，温暖的
always   *adv.* 总是
north   *n.* 北方

east *n.* 东方

wet *adj.* 潮湿的

west *n.* 西方

south *n.* 南方

season *n.* 季节

best *adv.* 最

night *n.* 夜晚

rise *v.* 升起

early *adv.* 早

set *v.* （太阳）落下去

late *adv.* 晚，迟

interesting *adj.* 有趣的，有意思的

subject *n.* 话题

conversation *n.* 谈话

Lesson 52

What nationality are they?
他们是哪国人？

I New words 新单词

1. **Australia** *n.* 澳大利亚

> Australia *n.* 澳大利亚
> Australia Internet providers 澳大利亚国际互联网
>   （Internet）供应商

She will spend her holiday in _____.

2. **Australian** *n.* 澳大利亚人

> Australian *n.* 澳大利亚人
> Australian Rules football 澳式橄榄球
> Australian crawl 澳大利亚式爬泳（两次打腿）

Have you ever heard the song "We are _____"?

3. **Austria** *n.* 奥地利
Don't confuse Austria with _____.

4. **Austrian** *n.* 奥地利人

> Austrian *n.* 奥地利人
> Austrian Corsican pine 南欧黑松

The _____ speaks German.

5. **Canada** *n.* 加拿大

> Canada   *n.* 加拿大
> Canada goose   加拿大黑雁，黑额黑雁

_____ produces good wheat.

6. **Canadian**   *n.* 加拿大人

> Canadian   *n.* 加拿大人
> Canadian patent   加拿大专利

She is a French _____.

7. **China**   *n.* 中国

> China   *n.* 中国
> Chinese   *n. & adj.* 汉语；中国的，中国人的

He reads "_____ Daily" every day.

8. **Finland**   *n.* 芬兰

> Finland   *n.* 芬兰
> Finlandize   *v.* 使芬兰化

The ship is bound for _____.

9. **Finnish**   *n.* 芬兰人

> Finnish   *n.* 芬兰人
> Finlander   *n.* 芬兰人

Can you speak _____?

10. **India**   *n.* 印度

> India   *n.* 印度
> India ink   中国及日本所用的墨，墨汁
> India paper   圣经纸，中国等地拓印版画所用之纸·

Her mother believes in _____ Buddhism.

11. **Indian**   *n.* 印度人

Indian   *n.* 印度人
Indian elephant   印度象，亚洲象
Indian Ocean   印度洋

Our neighbor is an _____.

12. **Japan**   *n.* 日本

Japan   *n.* 日本
Japanese   *n. & adj.* 日语；日本的，日本人的

I've never been to _____.

13. **Nigeria**   *n.* 尼日利亚
What is the postage to _____?

14. **Nigerian**   *n.* 尼日利亚人
Do you know any _____?

15. **Turkey**   *n.* 土耳其

Turkey   *n.* 土耳其
Turkey carpet   土耳其地毯
Turkey cock   火鸡，吐绶鸡
Turkey red   鲜红色，鲜红色棉布

_____ is a European country.

16. **Turkish**   *n.* 土耳其人

Turkish   *n.* 土耳其人
Turkish coffee   土耳其咖啡
Turkish tobacco   土耳其烟草

He ordered a cup of _____ coffee.

17. **Korea**   *n.* 韩国

> Korea   *n.* 韩国
>
> Korean   *n. & adj.* 韩国人，韩语，韩国的

That car is made in _____.

18. **Polish**   *n.* 波兰人

    The _____ speaks Slavic.

19. **Poland**   *n.* 波兰

    _____ is renowned for its multifarious types of delicious bread.

20. **Thai**   *n.* 泰国人

    Bangkok is the capital of _____.

21. **Thailand**   *n.* 泰国

    She likes the folk dance of _____.

Ⅱ Make sentences using the under-mentioned words 单词造句

Austria — Austrian

_____.

Australian — Australia

_____.

Canadian — Canada

_____.

China — Japan

_____.

Finland — Finnish

_____.

India — Indian

_____.

Nigeria — Nigerian

Turkey — Turkish

Korea — Korean

Polish- — Poland

Thai — Thailand

III Match 连线

- the smallest continent in the world
- a European country whose capital is Vienna
- the people or the language of Australia
- a country in North America whose capital is Ottawa
- the people of Austria
- the biggest country in Southeast Asia whose capital is Beijing
- people who are born in or live in Canada
- a country in Southeast Asia whose capital is New Delhi
- a northern European country
- the people of Finland
- a country in the Midwest of Africa
- the people of Nigeria
- the people of India
- a country in the northeastern part of Asia whose capital is Tokyo
- the people of Poland
- the country which is on the peninsula between the yellow sea and the Sea of Japan

Austria
Australian
Austrian
Australia
Canadian
Canada

China
Finland

Finnish
India
Indian
Japan
Nigeria
Nigerian

Turkey
Turkish

- country in the Middle East   Korea
- the people and the language of Turkey   Thai
- a Southeast Asian country whose capital is Bangkok   Poland
- a country in the middle of Europe   Thai
- the people of Thailand   Polish

Ⅳ *Glossary* 词汇表

Australia   *n.* 澳大利亚

Australian   *n.* 澳大利亚人

Austria   *n.* 奥地利

Austrian   *n.* 奥地利人

Canada   *n.* 加拿大

Canadian   *n.* 加拿大人

China   *n.* 中国

Finland   *n.* 芬兰

Finnish   *n.* 芬兰人

India   *n.* 印度

Indian   *n.* 印度人

Japan   *n.* 日本

Nigeria   *n.* 尼日利亚

Nigerian   *n.* 尼日利亚人

Turkey   *n.* 土耳其

Turkish   *n.* 土耳其人

Korea   *n.* 韩国

Polish   *n.* 波兰人

Poland   *n.* 波兰

Thai   *n.* 泰国人

Thailand   *n.* 泰国

The Sawyer family

索耶一家人

I New words 新单词

1. **live** *v.* 住，生活

> live *v.* 住，生活
> live in 住在一个比较大的地方（国家、城市）
> live at 住在一个比较小的地方（区、街道）

Fish can't _____ long out of water.

2. **stay** *v.* 呆在，停留

> stay *v.* 呆在，停留
> stay out 呆在户外
> stay at 暂住在，投宿在
> stay behind 留下来

The house has to _____ exactly at it was.

3. **home** *n. & adv.* 家；在家，到家

> home *n. & adv.* 家；在家，到家
> family *n.* 家庭，家族，家属
> stay at home 呆在家

They have a comfortable _____.

4. **housework** *n.* 家务

> housework   *n.* 家务
> do the housework   做家务活
> homework   *n.* 家庭作业

She dislikes doing _____.

5. **lunch**   *n.* 午饭

> lunch   *n.* 午饭
> lunch box   饭盒，便当
> lunch break   午休时间

It's high time for _____.

6. **afternoon**   *n.* 下午

> afternoon   *n.* 下午
> afternoon tea   下午茶（45 点钟）
> afternoon market   后市

He is having his _____ tea.

7. **usually**   *adv.* 通常

> usually   *adv.* 通常
> usual   *adj.* 平常的，通常的，惯例的
> usualness   经常性，惯常

I _____ get up at 7 o'clock.

8. **together**   *adv.* 一起

> together   *adv.* 一起
> all together   一起
> in company with   一起
> drink tea together   一起喝茶

The children play _____ in the street.

9. **evening** *n.* 晚上

> evening *n.* 晚上
> evening college   夜大
> evening course   夜班
> evening dress   夜礼服
> evening paper   晚报

Do you have any appointment this _____?

10. **arrive** *v.* 到达

> arrive *v.* 到达
> arrive at   到达（小的地方），达到
> arrive in   到达（大的地方）
> get to   到达
> reach *v.* 到达

At last, the day of graduation _____.

11. **night** *n.* 夜间

> night *n.* 夜间
> at night   在夜里
> night-blind *adj.* 患夜盲症的
> night-life *n.* 夜生活，夜晚娱乐活动

Did you have a good sleep last _____?

Ⅱ Make sentences using the under-mentioned words 单词造句

live — together

_____.

stay — home

_____.

housework — like

_____.

lunch — afternoon

_____.

usually — evening

_____.

arrive — night

_____.

III Match 连线 . . . .

- remain in the same place or state   night
- place where one lives, esp. with one's family   arrive
- work that you do at your house, e. g. cleaning   evening
  and washing
- meal eat at midday   usually
- the period between noon and sunset   together
- in or into a group; one with another   afternoon
- in most cases; generally   lunch
- last part of the day and beginning of night   housework
- come to a place   home
- the time when it is dark because there is no light   stay
  from the sun

IV Glossary 词汇表 . . . .

live   *v.* 住，生活
stay   *v.* 呆在，停留
home   *n. & adv.* 家；在家，到家
housework   *n.* 家务
lunch   *n.* 午饭
afternoon   *n.* 下午

usually   *adv.* 通常
together   *adv.* 一起
evening   *n.* 晚上
arrive   *v.* 到达
night   *n.* 夜间

Lesson 54 An unusual day 不平常的一天

I New words 新单词

1. **o'clock** *adv.* 点钟

> o'clock *adv.* 点钟
> clock *n.* 时钟
> clock-watcher *n.* 混时间的人，老是看钟等下班的人

The negotiation will begin at 9 _____ .

2. **shop** *n.* 商店

> shop *n.* 商店
> store *n.* 商店，店铺；*v.* 储藏，储备
> shop assistant 店员，售货员
> shopping *n.* 购物

Her daughter is a _____ assistant.

3. **moment** *n.* 片刻，瞬间

> moment *n.* 片刻，瞬间
> at the moment 指眼前，此刻
> in a moment 立刻
> for a moment 一会儿，片刻
> momentary *adj.* 瞬间的，刹那间的

He will be here in a _____.

II. *Make sentences using the under-mentioned words* 单词造句

o'clock — time

_____ .

shop — moment

_____ .

III. Match 连线

- a very short duration
- of the clock, used in indicating the hour of a day
- a small place selling retail

o'clock
shop
moment

IV. Glossary 词汇表

o'clock   *adv.* 点钟

shop   *n.* 商店

moment   *n.* 片刻，瞬间

Lesson 55

Is that all?
就这些吗?

I New words 新单词

1. **envelope** *n.* 信封

> envelope *n.* 信封
> envelope cartridge 信封纸
> letter *n.* 信，字母

He tore the _____ open.

2. **writing paper** 信纸

> writing paper 信纸
> letter-paper *n.* 信纸
> writing board 书写板
> writing ink （书写用的）墨水

The _____ is used up.

3. **shop assistant** 售货员

> shop assistant 售货员
> salesman *n.* 售货员
> shop around 逛商店
> shop hours 营业时间

The _____ is still dressed in her work clothes.

4. **size** *n.* 尺寸，尺码，大小

size *n.* 尺寸，尺码，大小
special size 特大号
large size 大号
medium size 中号（均码）
small size 小号
pocket size 袖珍型
portable size 便携式的

The two shirts are the same _____.

5. **pad** *n.* 信笺簿

pad *n.* 信笺簿
scratchpad *n.* 便签簿

She writes down the telephone number on a _____.

6. **glue** *n.* 胶水

glue *n.* 胶水（不可数名词）
a glue of water 一瓶胶水
gum water 胶水
mucilage *n.* 胶水，（植物的）黏液

This _____ makes a firmer bond.

7. **chalk** *n.* 粉笔

chalk *n.* 粉笔
a piece of chalk 一根粉笔
a box of chalk 一盒粉笔

The teacher wrote on the blackboard with a piece of _____.

8. **change** *n.* 零钱，找给的钱

change *n.* 零钱，找给的钱
change funds 找换金
change into 兑换

I have no _____ with me.

envelope — writing paper

_____.

shop assistant — change

_____.

size — pad

_____.

glue — money

_____.

chalk — blackboard

_____.

III Match 连线

- a paper covers for a letter   shop assistant
- paper for writing letters on   envelope
- a person who works in a shop   writing paper
- money that you get when you have paid too   size
  much
- piece of the soft limestone which is white and   pad
  used for marking esp. on the blackboard
- how big or small something is; an exact   glue
  measurement
- some pieces of paper that are joined together   chalk
  at one end
- a thick liquid that you use for sticking things   change
  together

Ⅳ Glossary 词汇表

envelope   *n.* 信封

writing paper   信纸

shop assistant   售货员

size   *n.* 尺寸, 尺码, 大小

pad   *n.* 信笺簿

glue   *n.* 胶水

chalk   *n.* 粉笔

change   *n.* 零钱, 找给的钱

56 **A bad cold** 重感冒

I New words 新单词

1. **feel** *v.* 感觉

> feel   *v.* 感觉
> sense   *n.* 感觉，判断力；*v.* 感到，理解，认识
> perceive   *v.* 感知，感到
> feel ill   感觉病了
> look ill   看起来病了

I could _____ rain on my face.

2. **look**   *v.* 看（起来）

> look   *v.* 看（起来）
> look about   四处寻找，考虑，察看，四处观看
> look like   像……，似……，外表特征是
> seem   *vi.* 像是，似乎

That dog _____ dangerous.

3. **must**   *v.* 必须

> must   *v.* 必须
> need   *v. & n.* 必须；必要，必需品
> want   *n. & v.* 短缺，需要
> will   *v. & n.* 必须，愿意，将；意志，决心，遗嘱

I _____ shut the door, or the rain will come in.

4. **call**   *v.* 叫，请

> call   *v.* 叫，请
>
> cry   *v.* 叫，喊，哭
>
> ask   *v.* 问，询问
>
> shout   *v.* 呼喊，呼叫

Someone is _____ for help.

5. **doctor**   *n.* 医生

> doctor   *n.* 医生
>
> doctor oneself   自我治疗
>
> surgeon   *n.* 外科医生
>
> internist   *n.* 内科医生
>
> nurse   *n.* 护士

The _____ had a very full day.

6. **telephone**   *n.* 电话

> telephone   *n.* 电话
>
> phone   *n.* 电话，打电话
>
> telephoned telegram   电话电报
>
> telephone number   电话号码
>
> telephone book   电话号簿

We told him the news by _____.

7. **remember**   *v.* 记得，记住

> remember   *v.* 记得，记住
>
> remember of   记得，想起
>
> remembrance   *n.* 回想，记忆，问候，纪念品，记
> 忆力

I _____ he used to dress in a blue suit.

8. **mouth** *n.* 嘴

> mouth   *n.* 嘴
> mouth-watering   *adj.* 令人垂涎的
> mouth capsule   口囊
> mouth cavity   口腔
> mouth organ   口琴

You'd better keep your _____ shut.

9. **tongue** *n.* 舌头

> tongue   *n.* 舌头
> tongue piece   舌片
> tongue position   舌位
> tongue root   舌根
> mother tongue   母语，本国语

His mother _____ is German.

10. **bad** *adj.* 坏的，严重的

> bad   *adj.* 坏的，严重的
> bad cold   重感冒
> have a bad cold   得了重感冒
> bad-mannered   *adj.* 没礼貌的
> bad-tempered   *adj.* 脾气不好的

He's _____ at getting along with his fellows.

11. **cold** *n.* 感冒

> cold   *n.* 感冒
> catch a hold   感冒

_____ are infectious.

12. **news**　*n.* 消息

> news　*n.* 消息
> message　*n.* 消息，信息
> information　*n.* 消息，信息，资料

We listen to the _____ on the radio every day.

II　Make sentences using the under-mentioned words 单词造句

feel — news

_____.

look — must

_____.

call — telephone

_____.

doctor — remember

_____.

mouth — tongue

_____.

bad — cold

_____.

III　Match 连线

- speak loudly and clearly so that somebody who is far away can hear you

  feel

- a word that you use to tell somebody what to do or what is necessary

  look

- seem to be; appear

  must

- have a sensation and impression; perceive by touch

  call

- words that tell people about things that have just happened

  doctor

- illness leading to fever or pain in nose and throat   telephone
- not good or nice   remember
- the soft part inside your mouth that moves when you talk or eat   mouth
- the part of your face below your nose that you using for eating and speaking   tongue
- to keep or bear in memory   bad
- an instrument that you use for talking to somebody who is in another place   cold
- a person whose job is to make sick people well again   news

Ⅳ Glossary 词汇表

feel   *v.* 感觉

look   *v.* 看（起来）

must   *v.* 必须

call   *v.* 叫，请

doctor   *n.* 医生

telephone   *n.* 电话

remember   *v.* 记得，记住

mouth   *n.* 嘴

tongue   *n.* 舌头

bad   *adj.* 坏的，严重的

cold   *n.* 感冒

news   *n.* 消息

What's the matter with them? 他们怎么啦？ What must they do? 他们该怎么办？

I New words 新单词

1. **headache** *n.* 头痛

> headache *n.* 头痛
> headachy *adj.* 头痛的，令人头痛的

Aspirin will quell your _____.

2. **aspirin** *n.* 阿斯匹林

> aspirin *n.* 阿斯匹林
> take / have an aspirin 服／吃一片阿司匹林

_____ can reduce fever.

3. **earache** *n.* 耳痛

> earache *n.* 耳痛
> ear cup 耳机
> ear defender 护耳器
> ear-trumpet *n.* 助听筒，号角状助听器
> ear-piercing *adj.* 刺耳的

_____ means pain in the eardrum.

4. **toothache** *n.* 牙痛

> toothache　*n.* 牙痛
> toothbrush　*n.* 牙刷
> toothed　*adj.* 有……齿的，锯齿状的
> tooth root　牙根

A _____ can get you down.

5. **dentist** *n.* 牙医

> dentist　*n.* 牙医
> surgeon dentist　牙外科医生

His father is a famous _____ .

6. **stomachache** *n.* 胃痛

> stomachache　*n.* 胃痛
> stomach upset　肠胃不适，消化不良
> stomachic　*adj.* 健胃的
> stomach powder　健胃散

She pretended to have got a _____ after meal and sneaked out of washing dishes.

7. **medicine** *n.* 药

> medicine　*n.* 药
> medicine-chest　*n.* 药箱，药柜
> medicine cabinet　医药箱
> medicine dropper　医药用滴管

This medicine has worked for my _____ .

8. **temperature** *n.* 温度

> temperature　*n.* 温度
> temperature adjustment　调温
> temperature change　温度改变（变化）

Lesson 57 What's the matter with them? 他们怎么啦?

> temperature drop 温度下降, 温差
> have a temperature 发烧

The _____ gets very high in summer.

9. **flu** *n.* 流行性感冒

> flu *n.* 流行性感冒
> bird flu 禽流感

He's down with _____.

10. **measles** *n.* 麻疹

> measles *n.* 麻疹
> measly *adj.* 患麻疹的
> measles encephalitis 麻疹脑炎

The child is sickening for the _____.

11. **mumps** *n.* 腮腺炎

Their youngest boy has gone down with _____.

Ⅱ Make sentences using the under-mentioned words 单词造句

headache — temperature

_____.

aspirin — medicine

_____.

earache — doctor

_____.

toothache — dentist

_____.

stomachache — hospital

_____.

flu — bird

measles — child

mumps — children

Ⅲ Match 连线

- a pain in one's tooth   headache
- a pain in one's ear   aspirin
- a medicine that stops pain   earache
- a pain in one's head   toothache
- how hot or cold somebody or something is   dentist
- pills or special drinks that help you to get   stomachache
  better when you are ill
- a pain in one's stomachache   medicine
- a person whose job is to look after your teeth   temperature
- an illness that makes small red spots comes on   skin
  one's
- disease caused by a virus with painful   measles
  swelling in the neck
- influenza   mumps

Ⅳ Glossary 词汇表

headache   *n.* 头痛
aspirin   *n.* 阿斯匹林
earache   *n.* 耳痛
toothache   *n.* 牙痛
dentist   *n.* 牙医
stomachache   *n.* 胃痛

medicine   *n.* 药
temperature   *n.* 温度
flu   *n.* 流行性感冒
measles   *n.* 麻疹
mumps   *n.* 腮腺炎

Lesson 58

Thank you, doctor.
谢谢你,医生。

I New words 新单词

1. **better** *adj.* 形容词 well 的比较级

> better *adj.* 形容词 well 的比较级
> best *adj.* 形容词 well 的最高级

She'll be much _____ soon.

2. **certainly** *adv.* 当然

> certainly *adv.* 当然
> sure *adv.* 当然,的确
> of course 当然
> certain *adj. & pron.* 确定的,某一个,必然的;
>   某几个,某些

You may _____ join us.

3. **get up** 起床

> get up 起床
> go to bed 上床
> go to sleep 入睡,睡着

When do you usually _____?

4. **yet** *adv.* 还,仍

> yet   *adv.* 还，仍
> still   *adv.* 还，仍，依然如此
> yet once more   再一次

He has not come _____.

5. **rich**   *adj.* 油腻的

> rich   *adj.* 油腻的
> fat   *adj.* 油腻的，肥的，多脂肪的
> greasy   *adj.* 油腻的，油污的，含脂肪的

I don't like _____ food.

6. **food**   *n.* 食物

> food   *n.* 食物
> food grain   粮食
> food chain   食物链
> food habit   饮食习惯
> food poisoning   食物中毒

Milk is the natural _____.

7. **remain**   *v.* 保持，继续

> remain   *v.* 保持，继续
> maintain   *v.* 继续，维持
> keep   *v.* 保持，继续不断，保存

It will _____ cold for a couple of days.

II *Make sentences using the under-mentioned words* 单词造句

better — remain

_____.

certainly — get up

_____.

yet — come

_____ .

rich — food

_____ .

Ⅲ Match 连线

- still; although   better
- get out of bed   certainly
- without any doubt   get up
- more good; less ill   yet
- stay in the same way; not change   rich
- fat; greasy   food
- edible substances which maintain life   remain

Ⅳ Glossary 词汇表

better   *adj.* 形容词 well 的比较级

certainly   *adv.* 当然

get up   起床

yet   *adv.* 还，仍

rich   *adj.* 油腻的

food   *n.* 食物

remain   *v.* 保持，继续

Lesson 59

Don't... !

不要……!

1. **play** *v.* 玩

> play *v.* 玩
> play with 玩……（东西）
> play with matches 玩火柴

The children are _____ in the garden.

2. **match** *n.* 火柴

> match *n.* 火柴
> matchstick *n.* 火柴杆
> matchbox 火柴盒
> matchmaking *n.* 火柴制造
> matchmaker *n.* 火柴制造者

It is dangerous to play with _____.

3. **talk** *v.* 谈话

> talk *v.* 谈话
> talk show 谈话节目
> talk about 谈论
> converse *v.* 交谈，谈话，认识

We _____ about music all night.

4. **library** *n.* 图书馆

> library *n.* 图书馆
> library card 借书证
> library collection 图书馆收藏（量）
> library science 图书馆（管理）学

I often borrow books from the school _____ .

5. **drive** *v.* 开车

> drive *v.* 开车
> drive's license 驾驶执照
> drive away 赶走，开走
> drive home 开车送回家，使人理解

He _____ me to the station.

6. **so** *adv.* 如此地

> so *adv.* 如此地
> such *adv.* 如此地，这样地
> thus *adv.* 如此，这样，从而

She was _____ weary that she fell.

7. **quickly** *adv.* 快地

> quickly *adv.* 快地
> quick *adj.* 快的，迅速的
> quicken *v.* 加快，鼓舞，刺激，生长，加速
> quickness *n.* 急速，迅速地，尖锐化

Come here _____ .

8. **lean out of** 身体探出

> lean out of　身体探出
> lean out　探身出去
> lean over　弯下身子，俯身于……之上
> lean to　倾向，偏向
> lean upon　依靠

It is dangerous to _____ the window.

9. **break** *v.* 打破

> break　*v.* 打破
> smash　*v.* 打碎，粉碎
> break silence　打破沉默
> break the record　打破纪录

He _____ a leg in the accident.

10. **noise** *n.* 喧闹声

> noise　*n.* 喧闹声
> make a noise　弄出噪音，发出响声
> noise damage　噪声致害，噪声损害
> noise grade　噪声等级
> noisy　*adj.* 吵杂的，聒噪的

The engine of my car makes funny _____.

II Make sentences using the under-mentioned words 单词造句

play — match

_____.

talk — noise

_____.

library — drive

_____.

so — quickly

_____ .

break — lean out of

_____ .

III Match 连线

- a special short thin piece of wood that makes fire when you rub it on something rough   play
- have fun; do something to enjoy yourself   match
- a word that you use when you say how much, how big, etc., something is   talk
- control a car, bus, etc. and make it to go   library
- a room or building where you go to read or borrow books   drive
- speak with another, especially to exchange ideas   so
- a loud sound that you do not like   quickly
- make something go into smaller pieces by droping it or hitting it   lean out of
- make one's body out of a window   break
- fast; that takes little time   noise

IV Glossary 词汇表

play   *v.* 玩
match   *n.* 火柴
talk   *v.* 谈话
library   *n.* 图书馆
drive   *v.* 开车
so   *adv.* 如此地

quickly   *adv.* 快地

lean out of   身体探出

break   *v.* 打破

noise   *n.* 喧闹声

Lesson 60

Not a baby

不是小孩子

I New words 新单词

1. **Dad**   *n.* 爸

> Dad   *n.* 爸（儿语）
> Daddy   *n.* 爸爸
> father   *n.* 父亲

_____ is snoozing by the fire.

2. **key**   *n.* 钥匙

> key   *n.* 钥匙
> key ring   钥匙圈
> lock   *n.* 锁

He lost the _____ to his car.

3. **baby**   *n.* 婴儿

> baby   *n.* 婴儿
> infant   *n. & adj.* 婴儿，未成年人；婴儿的，幼稚的
> baby-car   *n.* 婴儿车
> babywear   *n.* 婴儿装

Some _____ cry during the night.

4. **hear**   *v.* 听见

> hear   *v.* 听见（强调听的结果）
> listen to   听（强调听的动作）
> hear about   听说，接到消息
> hear from   接到……的信，受……批评
> hear of   听说

Can you _____ the signal?

5. **enjoy**   *v.* 玩得快活

> enjoy   *v.* 玩得快活
> enjoyable   *adj.* 令人愉快的，可享受的
> enjoyably   *adv.* 可享乐地，愉快地，有趣地
> enjoyment   *n.* 享乐，快乐，享受乐事

She _____ herself in the vacation.

6. **yourself**   *pron.* 你自己

> yourself   *pron.* 你自己
> your   *pron.* 你的，你们的
> yourselves   *pron.* 你们自己

Did you buy _____ a gift?

7. **ourselves**   *pron.* 我们自己

> ourselves   *pron.* 我们自己
> myself   *pron.* 我自己

We went there _____.

8. **mum**   *n.* 妈妈

> mum   *n.* 妈妈
> mother   *n.* 母亲

What are you doing, _____.

Ⅱ Make sentences using the under-mentioned words 单词造句

dad — hear

_____ .

key — yourself

_____ .

baby — mum

_____ .

enjoy — ourselves

_____ .

Ⅲ Match 连线

- a very young child   Dad
- get sounds with your ears   key
- father   baby
- a piece of metal that opens or closes a lock   hear
- a word that shows the same people when that you   enjoy
  have just talked about
- mother   yourself
- like something very much   ourselves
- a word that shows "you" when I have just talked   mum
  about you

Ⅳ Glossary 词汇表

Dad   *n.* 爸（儿语）

key   *n.* 钥匙

baby   *n.* 婴儿

hear　*v.*　听见
enjoy　*v.*　玩得快活
yourself　*pron.*　你自己
ourselves　*pron.*　我们自己
mum　*n.*　妈妈

What's the time?

几点钟?

I New words 新单词

1. **myself** *pron.* 我自己

> myself *pron.* 我自己
> my *adj.* 我的

I saw it _____.

2. **themselves** *pron.* 他们自己

> themselves *pron.* 他们自己
> them *pron.* 他们

They built the house _____.

3. **himself** *pron.* 他自己

> himself *pron.* 他自己
> him *pron.* 他

He's feeling _____ again.

4. **herself** *pron.* 她自己

> herself *pron.* 她自己
> her *pron.* 她; *adj.* 她的

I'd like to speak to the doctor _____.

II Make sentences using the under-mentioned words 单词造句

myself — herself

_____.

themselves — himself

_____.

III Match 连线

- a word that shows the same woman or girl that you have just talked about
- a word that shows the same woman or girl that you have just talked about
- a word that shows the same people, animals or things that you have just talked about
- a word that shows the same person as the one who is speaking

myself

themselves

himself

herself

IV Glossary 词汇表

myself *pron.* 我自己
themselves *pron.* 他们自己
himself *pron.* 他自己
herself *pron.* 她自己

Lesson 62 The weekend

周末

I New words 新单词

1. **greengrocer** *n.* 蔬菜水果零售商

> greengrocer　*n.* 蔬菜水果零售商
> greengrocer's（shop）　*n.* 蔬菜水果店

His father intended to set him up as a _____.

2. **absent** *adj.* 缺席的

> absent　*adj.* 缺席的
> beabsentfrom　不在，缺席
> be absent from school　缺课
> be absentfrom work　旷工

He is _____ from Hong Kong.

3. **Monday** *n.* 星期一
The delegation will arrive on _____ morning.

4. **Tuesday** *n.* 星期二
Tomorrow is _____.

5. **Wednesday** *n.* 星期三
She has _____ off.

6. **Thursday** *n.* 星期四
We'll have a meeting next _____.

7. **keep**   *v.*（身体健康）处于（状况），保持

> keep   *v.*（身体健康）处于（状况），保持
> maintain   *v.* 保持，维持，保养

He would not be able to _____ his job.

8. **spend**   *v.* 度过

> spend   *v.* 度过
> cost   *v.* 花费，付代价
> sth. cost sb. some money

I hope that you wouldn't _____ so much time watching television.

9. **weekend**   *n.* 周末

> weekend   *n.* 周末
> weekender   *n.* 周末旅行度假的人，周末屋
> weekend bag   周末旅行袋
> for the weekend   指整个周末这几天时间
> at the weekend   强调时间的某一点

We don't work at the _____.

10. **Friday**   *n.* 星期五

It may last till _____.

11. **Saturday**   *n.* 星期六

Are you free this _____?

12. **Sunday**   *n.* 星期日

I usually do some housework on _____.

13. **country**   *n.* 乡村

> country   *n.* 乡村
> village   *n.* 乡村，村庄；*adj.* 乡村的，乡村特点的

I prefer _____ life to life in the city.

14. **lucky** *adj.* 幸运的

> lucky　*adj.* 幸运的，碰巧的
>
> luck　*n.* 运气，好运，幸运
>
> luckily　*adv.* 幸运地，幸好

She was _____ to get such a well-paid job.

Ⅱ Make sentences using the under-mentioned words 单词造句

greengrocer — Sunday

_____.

absent — Monday

_____.

Tuesday — Wednesday

_____.

Thursday-Friday

_____.

keep-lucky

_____.

spend-weekend

_____.

country-life

_____.

Ⅲ Match 连线

- the third day of the week   greengrocer
- the second day of the week   absent
- not present   Monday

- a person who sells fruit and vegetables in a small shop　　　　　　　　　　Tuesday
- use time or money for something　　　Wednesday
- maintain　　　　　　　　　　　　　Thursday
- the fourth day of the week　　　　　keep
- the fifth day of the week　　　　　　spend
- the first day of the week　　　　　　weekend
- sunday and Saturday　　　　　　　　Friday
- the first day of the week　　　　　　Saturday
- the day which follows Friday　　　　Sunday
- having, bring or resulting from good luck　　country
- a rural area　　　　　　　　　　　lucky

IV Glossary 词汇表

greengrocer　n. 蔬菜水果零售商

absent　adj. 缺席的

Monday　n. 星期一

Tuesday　n. 星期二

Wednesday　n. 星期三

Thursday　n. 星期四

keep　v.（身体健康）处于（状况），保持

spend　v. 度过

weekend　n. 周末

Friday　n. 星期五

Saturday　n. 星期六

Sunday　n. 星期日

country　n. 乡村

lucky　adj. 幸运的

Lesson 63

What's the time?

几点钟？

I New words 新单词

1. **church**   *n.* 教堂

> church   *n.* 教堂
> temple   *n.* 寺庙，殿堂，教堂
> church of England   英国国教
> churchgoer   经常到教堂做礼拜的人
> churchgoing   *n.* 上教堂做礼拜

Aunt Mary goes to _____ every Sunday.

2. **dairy**   *n.* 乳品店

> dairy   *n.* 乳品店
> dairy farm   乳牛场
> dairying   *n.* 乳品业
> dairymaid   *n.* 乳酪农场的女工

We bought milk at the _____.

3. **baker**   *n.* 面包师傅

> baker   *n.* 面包师傅
> bake   *v.* 烘烤
> bakehouse   *n.* 面包店

Her husband is a _____.

4. **grocer**   *n.* 食品杂货商

> grocer   *n.* 食品杂货商
> grocery   *n.* 食品杂货业
> groceryman   *n.* ＜美＞食品杂货商

That _____ always overcharges.

II Make sentences using the under-mentioned words 单词造句

church — Sunday

_____.

dairy — milk

_____.

baker — bread

_____.

grocer — food

_____.

III Match 连线

- person who sells food and various household supplies   church
- a person who makes and sells bread and cakes   dairy
- a structure for Christian worship   baker
- place where milk and its products are manufactured   grocer

IV Glossary 词汇表

church   *n.* 教堂
dairy   *n.* 乳品店
baker   *n.* 面包师傅
grocer   *n.* 食品杂货商

· 249 ·

Lesson 64 The car race 汽车比赛

I New words 新单词

1. **year** *n.* 年

> year   *n.* 年
> year by year   一年又一年地
> year after year   年复一年
> year-around   *adj.* 全年的

It is just a _____ since I arrived here.

2. **race** *n.* 比赛

> race   *n.* 比赛
> carrace   车赛
> in the race   *n.* 在比赛中
> at the race   在赛场上

She won the _____ finally.

3. **town** *n.* 城填

> town   *n.* 城填
> town center   镇中心
> town council   镇政会
> city   *n.* 城市

He was born in a small _____.

4. **crowd**　*n.* 人群

> crowd　*n.* 人群
>
> crowded　*adj.* 拥挤的

He sidled through the _____.

5. **stand**　*v.* 站立

> stand　*v.* 站立
>
> stand about　闲散的站着
>
> stand against　靠着……站立，抵挡，反对

They _____ because there were no seats.

6. **exciting**　*adj.* 使人激动的

> exciting　*adj.* 使人激动的
>
> excite　*v.* 刺激，使兴奋
>
> excited　*adj.* 激动的，兴奋的，活跃的

This is really an _____ news.

7. **just**　*adv.* 正好，恰好

> just　*adv.* 正好，恰好
>
> just as　正像，正当……时
>
> just as it is　恰好如此

That is _____ what I think.

8. **finish**　*n.* 结尾，结束

> finish　*n.* 结尾，结束
>
> finality　*n.* 结尾
>
> end　*n. & adj.* 末尾，结束，结局
>
> close　*v.* 关闭，终结，结束

At eleven the dinner finally dragged to a _____.

9. **winner** *n.* 获胜者

> winner *n.* 获胜者
> win *v.* 获胜
> winning *adj. & n.* 获胜的，胜利，赢得物
> winnable *adj.* 可获得的，可成功的

He's a real _____ .

10. **behind** *prep.* 在……之后

> behind *prep.* 在……之后
> behind one' back 在某人背后
> behind schedule 落后于预定计划，晚点
> behind the curtain 幕后，秘密
> back *adj. & adv.* 背后的，后面的，向后地，回
>   原处

He hangs his coat on the clothes rack _____ the door.

11. **way** *n.* 路途

> way *n.* 路途
> way of life 生活方式，生活准则
> way of production 生产方式
> road *n.* 道路，公路，街道
> on the way home/on one' way home 在回家的途中
> on the way 在……的途中

On the _____ , a young man waved to me.

Ⅱ *Make sentences using the under-mentioned words* 单词造句

year — race

_____

town — exciting

_____.

crowd — stand

_____.

just — behind

_____.

finish — winner

_____.

way — home

_____.

Ⅲ Match 连线

- a place where there are a lot of houses and buildings   year
- a lot of people together   race
- a time of 365 or 366 days from 1 Janaury to 31 december   town
- a competiton to see who can run, drive, ride, etc. fastest   crowd
- the last part of something; the end   stand
- at this or that moment   exciting
- something that makes you have strong feelings of happiness or interest   just
- be on your feet   finish
- at or to the back of something or somebody   winner
- a road or parth that you followed to go to a direction   behind
- a person or animal that wins a game, race or competition   way

IV *Glossary* 词汇表

year   *n.* 年

race   *n.* 比赛

town   *n.* 城填

crowd   *n.* 人群

stand   *v.* 站立

exciting   *adj.* 使人激动的

just   *adv.* 正好，恰好

finish   *n.* 结尾，结束

winner   *n.* 获胜者

behind   *prep.* 在……之后

way   *n.* 路途

Lesson 65

When were they there?
他们是什么时候在那里的？

I New words 新单词

1. **stationer** *n.* 文具商

> stationer *n.* 文具商
> stationery *n. & adj.* 文具，文具用品的
> pencil-box *n.* 文具盒

I have to go to the _____ 's to get some envelopes.

2. **Denmark** *n.* 丹麦

> Denmark *n.* 丹麦
> Danish *adj.* 丹麦人的，丹麦语的
> Dane *n.* 丹麦人

He will fly to _____ next month.

II Make sentences using the under-mentioned words 单词造句

stationer — pen

_____.

Danmark — travel

_____.

III Match 连线

- A European country
- A place where you can buy writing materials such as pens, papers and envelops etc

stationer
Denmark

IV Glossary 词汇表

stationer   *n.* 文具商
Denmark   *n.* 丹麦

Lesson
66

He's awful!
他讨厌透了！

I New words 新单词

1. **awful** *adj.* 让人讨厌的，坏的

> awful *adj.* 让人讨厌的，坏的
> offensive *adj.* 令人讨厌的，令人作呕的，无礼的
> awfully *adv.* 可怕地，极度地

That's an _____ book.

2. **telephone** *v. & n.* 打电话；电话

> telephone *v. & n.* 打电话；电话
> phone *v. & n.* 打电话，电话
> cellphone *n.* 手机

Please answer the _____.

3. **time** *n.* 次（数）

> time *n.* 次（数）（可数名词）
> time *n.* 时间（不可数名词）
> time and again 屡次，反复

How many _____ have you read this book?

4. **answer** *v.* 接（电话）

> answer *v.* 接（电话）
> answer the door 应门，去开门

> answering machine　留言机
> answering service　代接电话服务站

She is _____ the telephone.

5. **last** *adj.* 最后的，前一次的

> last　*adj.* 最后的，前一次的
> last minute　最后一刻，紧急关头
> last night　昨晚
> last month　上个月

He was the very _____ to leave the office.

6. **phone** *n.* 电话（=telephone）

> phone　*n.* 电话（=telephone）
> mobile phone　手机

You just bought a new mobile _____ , didn't you?

7. **again** *adv.* 又一次地

> again　*adv.* 又一次地
> again and again　再三地，反复地

Please say that _____.

8. **say**（said）　*v.* 说

> say（said）　*v.* 说
> speak　*v.* 说话，演讲
> talk　*v.* 谈话
> tell　*v.* 告诉

It's hard to _____ who is right in this matter.

Ⅱ *Make sentences using the under-mentioned words* 单词造句

awful — last

_____.

telephone-answer

_____.

time-many

_____.

phone-again

_____.

say-what

_____.

III Match 连线

- pick up the telephone when it rings, and spaeak   awful
- a certain moment or occasion   telephone
- an instrument that you use for talking to sb.   time
  who is in another place
- very bad   answer
- make words with your mouth   last
- one more time; once more   phone
- a telephone   again
- after all the others; just before now   say (said)

IV Glossary 词汇表

> awful   *adj.* 让人讨厌的，坏的
> telephone   *v. & n.* 打电话；电话
> time   *n.* 次（数）
> answer   *v.* 接（电话）
> last   *adj.* 最后的，前一次的
> phone   *n.* 电话（=telephone）
> again   *adv.* 又一次地
> say (said)   *v.* 说

Lesson 67

The way to King Street
到国王街的走法

I New words 新单词

1. week *n.* 周

> week *n.* 周
> the week before last　上上周
> the week after next　下下周

I play tennis twice a _____.

2. London *n.* 伦敦

> London *n.* 伦敦
> London fog　伦敦雾
> London smoke　伦敦烟灰色，暗灰色

He has lived in _____ for 3 years.

3. suddenly *adv.* 突然地

> suddenly　*adv.* 突然地
> sudden　*adj.* 突然的，忽然的
> suddenness　*n.* 突然，意外

An accident happened _____.

4. bus stop 公共汽车站

> bus stop　公共汽车站
> station　*n.* 车站，驻地，职位

Where's the nearest _____?

5. **smile**   *v.* 微笑

> smile   *v.* 微笑
> laugh   *n. & v.* 笑；发笑

She _____ when she saw me.

6. **pleasantly**   *adv.* 愉快地

> pleasantly   *adv.* 愉快地
> pleasant   *adj.* 愉快的
> pleasant-voiced   *adj.* 说话令人悦耳的

He accepted this task _____.

7. **understand**   (understood)   *v.* 懂，明白

> understand (understood)   *v.* 懂，明白
> clear about   明白
> know   *v.* 懂得，知晓，了解

I don't _____ what you mean.

8. **speak**   (spoke)   *v.* 讲，说

> speak (spoke)   *v.* 讲，说
> tell   *v.* 说，告诉
> say   *v.* 讲话，说话，讲述

Can your child _____ yet?

9. **hand**   *n.* 手

> hand   *n.* 手
> shake hands with... 和……握手
> hand in hand   手牵手

They shake _____ with each other.

10. **pocket** *n.* 衣袋

> pocket *n.* 衣袋
> bag *n.* 包

My keys are in my coat _____.

11. **phrasebook** *n.* 短语手册，常用语手册

> phrasebook *n.* 短语手册，常用语手册
> phrase marker 短语标记
> phrase structure 短语结构

She always takes a _____ with her.

12. **phrase** *n.* 短语

> phrase *n.* 短语
> phrasemaker *n.* 善于创造警句的人
> phrasal *adj.* 短语的，成语的

Try to remember these English words and _____.

13. **slowly** *adv.* 缓慢地

> slowly *adv.* 缓慢地
> slow *adj.* 慢的，缓慢的

Can you speak _____?

Ⅱ *Make sentences using the under-mentioned words* 单词造句

week — suddenly

_____.

London — bus stop

_____.

smile — pleasantly

_____.

speak-understand

_____.

hand-pocket

_____.

phrasebook-phrase

_____.

slowly-walk

_____.

III Match 连线

- a place where buses stop and people get on and off   week

- happening quickly and without warning   London

- name of a period of seven days   suddenly

- capital of Britain   bus stop

- utter words; talk   smile

- to take or grasp the meaning or importance of something   pleasantly

- move your moiuth to show that you are happy   understand (understood)

- enjoyably or friendly   speak (spoke)

- a pamphlet collected with phrases   hand

- a group bof words that you use together as part of a sentence   pocket

- not quickly   phrasebook

- end part of the arm, blow the wrist   phrase

- small bag in or on garment   slowly

IV Glossary 词汇表

week *n.* 周
London *n.* 伦敦
suddenly *adv.* 突然地
bus stop 公共汽车站
smile *v.* 微笑
pleasantly *adv.* 愉快地
understand（understood） *v.* 懂，明白
speak（spoke） *v.* 讲，说
hand *n.* 手
pocket *n.* 衣袋
phrasebook *n.* 短语手册，常用语手册
phrase *n.* 短语
slowly *adv.* 缓慢地

Lesson 68

What did they do?

他们干了什么?

I New words 新单词

1. **hurriedly** *adv.* 匆忙地

> hurriedly *adv.* 匆忙地
> hurry *n.* 匆忙，仓促
> hurried *adj.* 匆忙的，仓促的

He pushed me aside and left _____.

2. **cut** (cut) *v.* 割，切

> cut (cut) *v.* 割，切
> cut a long story short 简而言之
> cut across 抄近路通过

She _____ the birthday cake with a knife.

3. **thirstily** *adv.* 口渴地

> thirstily *adv.* 口渴地
> thirst *n. & v.* 口渴，渴望
> thirstless *adj.* 不渴的
> thirsty *adj.* 渴的，渴望的

The soldiers drank _____ from the bottle that was passed around.

4. **go** (went) *v.* 走

> go（went） v. 走
> come v. 来
> go away 走开，离去
> go out 出去，离开
> go for a walk 去散步

Let's _____ out for a walk! 咱们出去散散步吧!

5. **greet** v. 问候，打招呼

> greet v. 问候，打招呼
> greeting n. 问候，迎接，招呼
> greeting card 贺卡

She rose to _____ her guests.

II Make sentences using the under-mentioned words 单词造句

hurriedly — go（went）

_____.

cut-hand

_____.

thirsty-water

_____.

greet-guests

_____.

III Match 连线

- express welcome, friendliness, respect, etc. to   hurriedly
- move or intended to move; proceed   cut（cut）
- take one piece from something bigger   thirstily
- do something in a hurry   go（went）
- feel thirsty   greet

Ⅳ Glossary 词汇表

hurriedly　*adv.* 匆忙地

cut（cut）　*v.* 割，切

thirstily　*adv.* 口渴地

go（went）　*v.* 走

greet　*v.* 问候，打招呼

Lesson 69

Uncomfortable shoes
不舒适的鞋子

I New words 新单词

1. **ago** *adv.* 以前

   > ago   *adv.* 以前
   > before   *adv.* & *prep.* 以前，过去

   I went to London three days _____.

2. **buy** （bought） *v.* 买

   > buy （bought） *v.* 买
   > buy back   买回
   > buy up   全部买下
   > sell   *v.* 卖

   I _____ a coat in Paris last month.

3. **pair** *n.* 双，对

   > pair   *n.* 双，对
   > a pair of   一双，一对

   The dressmaker cuts cloth with a _____ of scissors.

4. **fashion** *n.* （服装的）流行式样

   > fashion   *n.* （服装的）流行式样
   > be in fashion   流行的，时髦的
   > be out of fashion   不流行的

Her dress is the latest _____ .

5. **uncomfortable**   *adj.* 不舒服的

> uncomfortable   *adj.* 不舒服的
> comfortable   *adj.* 舒服的

She feels _____ in tight boots.

6. **wear**   （wore） *v.* 穿着

> wear（wore） *v.* 穿着
> put on   穿
> dress   *v.* 给……穿衣服，使穿上

The lady is _____ a beautiful dress.

II Make sentences using the under-mentioned words 单词造句

ago — buy

_____ .

pair — uncomfortable

_____ .

wear — fashion

_____ .

III Match 连线

- to have some garments covering one's body   ago
- a popular style of dressing   buy（bought）
- give money to others in exchange for things   pair
  or goods
- not comfortable   fashion
- tow things which are similar in form or faction   uncomfortable

- in the past; gone by   wear (wore)

Ⅳ Glossary 词汇表

ago   *adv.* 以前
buy (bought)   *v.* 买
pair   *n.* 双，对
fashion   *n.* （服装的）流行式样
uncomfortable   *adj.* 不舒服的
wear (wore)   *v.* 穿着

Lesson 70

Terrible toothache
要命的牙痛

I New words 新单词

1. **appointment** *n.* 约会，预约

> appointment *n.* 约会，预约
> have an appointment（with sb.）（与某人）有约
>   会/预约
> make anappointment　订个约会
> change anappointment　改约

Once you've make an _____, you should try to keep it.

2. **urgent** *adj.* 紧急的，急迫的

> urgent *adj.* 紧急的，急迫的
> urgency *n.* 紧急，急迫，紧急情况
> urgent committee　紧急委员会
> urgent dispatch　急件
> urgent need　急需

The children in that area are in _____ need of medical attention.

3. **till** *prep.* 直到……为止

> till *prep.* 直到……为止
> until *prep.* 直至……为止，直到……才（可用
>   于句首）

I'll be waiting for you _____ ten o'clock.

II Make sentences using the under-mentioned words 单词造句

appointment — urgent

_____.

till — midnight

_____.

III Match 连线

- requiring for immediate action   appointment
- up to a special time   urgent
- an arrangement to meet, interview or visit   till
  someone at a specifiedtime

IV Glossary 词汇表

appointment   *n.* 约会，预约

urgent   *adj.* 紧急的，急迫的

till   *prep.* 直到……为止

Lesson 71

Carol's shopping list
卡罗尔的购物单

I New words 新单词

1. **shopping** *n.* 购物

> shopping　*n.* 购物
> make a shoppinglist　写一张采购物品的单子
> go shopping　去购物
> do some shopping　购物
> shopping center　购物中心
> shopping mall　商业街区

_____ online is very convenient.

2. **list** *n.* 单子

> list　*n.* 单子
> price list　价格表
> listed　*adj.* 记录在表格上的
> list of award　决算表
> list of resources　资产清单

This is the price _____ of our products.

3. **vegetable** *n.* 蔬菜

> vegetable　*n.* 蔬菜
> vegetable butter　植物脂

> vegetable kingdom　植物界
> vegetable marrow　西葫芦
> vegetable plate　蔬菜拼盘

I ordered a plate of _____ salad.

4. **need**　*v.* 需要

> need　*v.* 需要
> in need　在困难中，在危难中
> in need of　需要
> need time for　需要时间做……

My shirt _____ a button.

5. **hope**　*v.* 希望

> hope　*v.* 希望
> hopeful　*adj.* 充满希望的，有前途的
> hopeless　*adj.* 绝望的，不抱希望的
> in the hope of　怀着……的希望，期待着
> hope to do sth. / hope that　希望

I _____ to study abroad next year.

6. **thing**　*n.* 事情

> thing　*n.* 事情
> thingy　*adj.* 物质的，实际的
> matter　*n.* 事情，物质，问题，材料

I have many _____ on my mind.

7. **money**　*n.* 钱

> money　*n.* 钱
> money bill　财政法案
> money-box　*n.* 储存盒，募捐箱
> money capital　货币资本

_____ doesn't always bring happiness.

II Make sentences using the under-mentioned words 单词造句

shopping — list

_____.

vegetable — money

_____.

need — hope

_____.

thing — bad

_____.

III Match 连线

- require; want   shopping
- plant grown for food   list
- series of names, items, figures, etc. written or printed   vegetable
- buying things from shops   need
- what happens or what you do   hope
- coins and bank notes   thing
- to wish for something with expectation   money

IV Glossary 词汇表

shopping   *n.* 购物
list   *n.* 单子
vegetable   *n.* 蔬菜
need   *v.* 需要
hope   *v.* 希望
thing   *n.* 事情
money   *n.* 钱

Lesson 72

I must go to the...
我必须去……

I New words 新单词

1. **groceries** *n.* 食品杂货

> groceries *n.* 食品杂货
> grocer *n.* 食品杂货商
> grocery 食品杂货业，食品杂货店

She carries a basket of _____.

2. **fruit** *n.* 水果

> fruit *n.* 水果
> fruit salad 水果色拉
> fruit piece 果实的静物画
> fruit stall 水果摊，水果店

Would you like some _____?

3. **stationery** *n.* 文具

> stationery *n.* 文具
> stationer *n.* 文具商

The shop that sells _____ is called a stationer's.

4. **newsagent** *n.* 报刊零售人

> newsagent *n.* 报刊零售人
> newspaper *n.* 新闻，报刊
> newsstand *n.* 报摊

You can get that newspaper at your local _____.

5. chemist   *n.* 药剂师

> chemist   *n.* 药剂师
> chemistry   *n.* 化学，化学反应及现象
> chemical   *adj.* 化学的

He is acknowledged as an outstanding _____.

II Make sentences using the under-mentioned words 单词造句

groceries — fruit

_____.

stationery — stationer

_____.

newsagent — chemist

_____.

III Match 连线

- a person who studies chemistry or makes and sells medicines
- paper, pens and other things you use for writing
- a person who has a shop that sells newspapers
- food and various household things
- a ripened, seed-bearing plant

groceries

fruit

stationery

newsagent

chemist

IV Glossary 词汇表

> groceries   *n.* 食品杂货
> fruit   *n.* 水果
> stationery   *n.* 文具
> newsagent   *n.* 报刊零售人
> chemist   *n.* 药剂师

Lesson 73

Roast beef and potatoes
烤牛肉和土豆

I New words 新单词 ....

1. **bath**   *n*. 洗澡

> bath   *n*. 洗澡
> have (take) a bath   洗澡
> bath gown   浴衣
> bathe   *v*. 沐浴

I'm used to having a _____ every day.

2. **nearly**   *adv*. 几乎，将近

> nearly   *adv*. 几乎，将近
> almost   *adv*. 几乎，差不多，将近

I _____ missed the train. 我差点儿错过那趟火车。

3. **ready**   *adj*. 准备好的，完好的

> ready   *adj*. 准备好的，完好的
> get ready for/be ready for   准备好……，为……
>   准备好
> ready box   备用弹药箱
> ready cash   现金

We must get the house _____ for our guests.

4. **dinner**   *n*. 正餐，晚餐

· 278 ·

> dinner　*n.*　正餐，晚餐
> dinner bucket　（工人用的）饭盒
> dinner party　宴会
> dinner service　（一套）西餐具

Shall we have chicken or duck for _____ ?

5. **restaurant**　*n.*　饭馆，餐馆

> restaurant　*n.*　饭馆，餐馆
> restaurateur　*n.*　餐馆老板
> hotel　*n.*　饭店，旅馆，旅社

Trains usually have a _____ car.

6. **roast**　*adj.*　烤的

> roast　*adj.*　烤的
> roast sucking pig　烤乳猪
> roaster　*n.*　烘烤者，烘烤器，适合烘烤的食物
> roasting　*adj.*　用于烘焙的，灼热的；*n.* 烤，炙

Help yourself to some _____ duck!

II Make sentences using the under-mentioned words 单词造句

bath — tired

_____.

nearly — restaurant

_____.

ready — dinner

_____.

roast — duck

_____.

III Match 连线

- cook or be cooked in an oven or over a fire   bath
- main meal of the day, usually eaten in the evening   nearly
- place where meal is bought and eaten   ready
- washing one's body in a bath   dinner
- prepared for action or use   restaurant
- almost; not quite   roast

IV Glossary 词汇表

bath   *n.* 洗澡

nearly   *adv.* 几乎，将近

ready   *adj.* 准备好的，完好的

dinner   *n.* 正餐，晚餐

restaurant   *n.* 饭馆，餐馆

roast   *adj.* 烤的

I had...
我吃（喝、从事）了……

I New words 新单词

1. **breakfast** *n.* 早饭

> breakfast *n.* 早饭
> lunch *n.* 午餐
> dinner *n.* 晚餐

He seldom eats _____.

2. **haircut** *n.* 理发

> haircut *n.* 理发
> hairdo *n.* （尤指女子的）发式
> hairdress *v.* 做头发

I'll go and get a _____ this evening.

3. **party** *n.* 聚会

> party *n.* 聚会
> birthday party 生日聚会
> party girl 派对女郎

I'd like to invite you to attend my birthday _____.

4. **holiday** *n.* 假日

> holiday *n.* 假日
> on holiday/on one's holidays 度假
> vacation *n.* 休假，休息，假期

When I was on _____ , I visited my uncle.

II Make sentences using the under-mentioned words 单词造句

breakfast — bread

_____.

haircut — long

_____.

party — holiday

_____.

III Match 连线

- day of rest from work   breakfast
- social gathering   haircut
- the first meal of a day, usually eaten in the morning   party
- when somebody cuts your hair   holiday

IV Glossary 词汇表

> breakfast   *n.* 早饭
> haircut   *n.* 理发
> party   *n.* 聚会
> holiday   *n.* 假日

Lesson 75　Going on holiday

度假

1. **mess**　*n.* 杂乱，凌乱

> mess　*n.* 杂乱，凌乱
> Excuse the mess　屋子很乱，请原谅
> mess-up　*n.* 一团糟，混乱

What a _____ !

2. **pack**　*v.* 打包，装箱

> pack　*v.* 打包，装箱
> pack away　收藏
> pack off　打发走，离开
> pack up　整理行装，收拾行李
> pack one's suitcase　打包，收拾行李

They _____ their bags and left.

3. **suitcase**　*n.* 手提箱

> suitcase　*n.* 手提箱
> suit　*n.* 衣服，全套衣服
> case　*n.* 箱子

A _____ is enough to take your clothes with you on holiday.

4. **leave**　*v.* 离开

leave *v.* 离开
leave for 动身到
on leave 休假
take one's leave 告辞

The train is going to _____ in 5 minutes.

5. **already** *adv.* 已经

already *adv.* 已经
yet *adv.* 迄今，仍然，还
still *adv.* 还，仍然

She had _____ gone when I arrived.

II *Make sentences using the under-mentioned words* 单词造句

mess — room

_____.

pack — suitcase

_____.

leave — already

_____.

III Match 连线

- go away from   mess
- by this time; before now   pack
- a state of untidiness or dirt   suitcase
- to put things into a case for travelling or storing   leave
- case with flat sides, usually for carrying clothes,   already
  etc. when traveling

Ⅳ Glossary 词汇表

mess   *n.* 杂乱，凌乱
pack   *v.* 打包，装箱
suitcase   *n.* 手提箱
leave   *v.* 离开
already   *adv.* 已经

Paris in the spring
巴黎之春

Ⅰ New words 新单词 ....

1. **Paris** *n.* 巴黎

> Paris *n.* 巴黎
> Paris doll （女服装店的）人体模特
> Paris green 巴黎绿
> Paris white 巴黎白，白粉，亮粉

They honeymooned in _____.

2. **cinema** *n.* 电影院

> cinema *n.* 电影院
> cinemagoer *n.* 常去看电影的人
> cinematic *adj.* 电影院的，影片的，电影艺术的

Smoking is forbidden in _____.

3. **film** *n.* 电影

> film *n.* 电影
> filmdom *n.* 电影界，电影业
> filmscript *n.* 电影剧本
> filmfest *n.* 电影节
> movie *n.* 电影，影片

Have you seen any good _____ lately?

4. **beautiful** *adj.* 漂亮的

> beautiful *adj.* 漂亮的
> beauty *n.* 美丽，美感
> beautify *v.* 美化

She was even more _____ than I had expected.

5. **city** *n.* 城市

> city *n.* 城市
> metropolis *n.* 大都市
> urban *adj.* 城市的

Weihai is an ideal _____ for living.

6. **never** *adv.* 从来没有

> never *adv.* 从来没有
> never-ending *adj.* 永无止境的，永远的
> never heard of it 从来没听说过
> never mind 别担心，别介意

"_____ too old to Learn" is an idiom.

7. **ever** *adv.* 在任何时候

> ever *adv.* 在任何时候
> ever-present *adj.* 始终存在的，总是在场的
> ever since 自从

It was the best result they've _____ had.

II *Make sentences using the under-mentioned words* 单词造句

Paris — beautiful

_____.

cinema — film

_____.

city — ever

_____.

never — change

_____.

III Match 连线

- at all times; always   Paris
- at no time; not at all   cinema
- a large important town   film
- a place where is enclosed and films are shown   beautiful
- of the quality that delights the eye, ear or mind   city
- movie   never
- apital of France   ever

IV Glossary 词汇表

Paris   *n.* 巴黎
cinema   *n.* 电影院
film   *n.* 电影
beautiful   *adj.* 漂亮的
city   *n.* 城市
never   *adv.* 从来没有
ever   *adv.* 在任何时候

77

A car crash

车祸

I New words 新单词

1. **attendant** *n.* 接待员

> attendant *n.* 接待员
> attendance *n.* 看护，出席，侍从
> attend *v.* 照顾，照料，出席

The _____ asked if I need her help.

2. **bring** (**brought/brought**) *v.* 带来，送来

> bring (brought/brought) *v.* 带来，送来
> bring along 随身携带
> bring back 拿回来，使恢复
> bring in 引来，吸收
> take *v.* 带走，拿走

You are welcome to _____ your wife to the party.

3. **garage** *n.* 车库，汽车修理厂

> garage *n.* 车库，汽车修理厂
> garageman *n.* 汽车修理工人

The _____ is outside the door.

4. **crash** *n.* 碰撞

crash　*n.* 碰撞
a car crash　汽车相撞
crash into　碰撞，坠毁
have a crash　碰（撞）车

She survived the plane _____.

5. **lamp-post**　*n.* 灯杆，路灯柱

lamp-post　*n.* 灯杆，路灯柱
lamp chimney　玻璃灯罩
lamp holder　灯座，洋台灯
lamp oil　灯油

The _____ was blown down last night.

6. **repair**　*v.* 修理

repair　*v.* 修理
mend　*v.* 修理，修补，改良
repairable　*adj.* 可修理的
repairer　*n.* 修理工人，修补者

She looked into the mirror and began to _____ her face.

7. **try**　*v.* 努力，设法

try　*v.* 努力，设法
try to do sth.　试着做某事
have a try　试一下

He is _____ to move the book shelf.

Ⅱ *Make sentences using the under-mentioned words* 单词造句

bring — garage

_____.

crash — lamp — post

_____ .

repair — try

_____ .

III Match 连线

- make effort to do something which one has not done before
- to restore to good condition after injury, damage or wear
- a tall thing in the street with a light in the top
- come to a place with somebody or something
- a building where you keep your car or make your car mended
- cause something to have collision

bring (brought/ brought)

garage

crash

lamp-post

repair

try

IV Glossary 词汇表

attendent   *n.* 接待员

bring (brought/brought)   *v.* 带来，送来

garage   *n.* 车库，汽车修理厂

crash   *n.* 碰撞

lamp-post   *n.* 灯杆，路灯柱

repair   *v.* 修理

try   *v.* 努力，设法

For sale

待售

1. **believe** *v.* 相信，认为

> believe *v.* 相信，认为
> believe in 相信
> make believe 假装
> belief *n.* 信仰，信任，信心

I don't _____ you.

2. **may** *v.* 可以

> may *v.* 可以
> can *v.* 可能，能够，可以
> may I...? 我可以……? (是一种比较正式的表示请求的句型)
> maybe 大概，可能

You _____ come if you wish.

3. **how long** 多长

> how long 多长
> how wide 多宽
> how high 多高

_____ can I stay here?

4. **since** *prep.* 自从

> since　*prep.*　自从
> ever since　从那以后（一直）
> since then　自那以后
> long since　好久以前

They have been friends _____ childhood.

5. **why** *adv.* 为什么

> why　*adv.*　为什么
> why not...?　何不……?（提建议）

I can't tell you _____ she is crying.

6. **sell** *v.* 卖，出售

> sell　*v.*　卖，出售
> sold　sell 的过去式、过去分词
> sell out　完
> sell off　贱价卖掉

She _____ her old bicycle to me.

7. **because** *conj.* 因为

> because　*conj.*　因为
> because of　因为，由于

I do it _____ I like it.

8. **retire** *v.* 退休

> retire　*v.*　退休
> retirement　*n.*　退休，引退

He's going to _____ soon from the sea.

9. **cost** *v.* 花费

> cost *v.* 花费
> worth *n.* 价值

The coat _____ $ 30.

10. **pound** *n.* 英镑（£）

> pound *n.* 英镑（£）
> a pound of flesh 合法但极不合理的要求
> penny wise and pound foolish 小事聪明，小事糊涂

He bought a car for five hundred _____.

11. **worth** *prep.* 值得

> worth *prep.* 值得
> worthless *adj.* 无价值的，无用的
> worthy *adj.* 值得的，有价值的
> worthwhile *adj.* 值得花精力或时间的
> be worth doing 值得……

The book is _____ reading.

12. **penny** *n.* 便士

> penny *n.* 便士
> in for a penny, in for a word 一不做，二不休
> earn an honest penny 用正当的手段挣一点钱
> pennies from the heaven 意外得到的好处

It won't cost a _____.

Ⅱ *Make sentences using the under-mentioned words* 单词造句

believe — retire

_____.

how long — since

_____.

why — because

_____.

sell — may

_____.

cost — pound

_____.

worth — penny

_____.

Ⅲ Match 连线

- during the period after, until now
- for what reason
- give (goods, etc.) to sb. who becomes their owner after paying one money
- for the reason that
- to stop working at one's job, profession, usually because of age
- a standard measure of weight equal to 454 kilograms
- the value of
- a small copper and tin coin, 100 of which make a pound
- feel sure that something is true or right
- the measurement of a period of time
- (used to show possibility) to be perhaps likely to
- the money you spend when you want to get or buy something

believe

may

how long

since

why

sell

because

retire

cost

pound

worth

penny

IV *Glossary* 词汇表

- believe *v.* 相信，认为
- may *v.* 可以
- how long 多长
- since *prep.* 自从
- why *adv.* 为什么
- sell *v.* 卖，出售
- because *conj.* 因为
- retire *v.* 退休
- cost *v.* 花费
- pound *n.* 英镑（£）
- worth *prep.* 值得
- penny *n.* 便士

Lesson 79

Poor Ian!

可怜的伊恩!

I New words 新单词

1. **still** *adv.* 还，仍旧

> still *adv.* 还，仍旧
> yet *adv.* 至今（还），仍然，还

I _____ don't understand what he meant.

2. **move** *v.* 搬家

> move *v.* 搬家
> move to 搬到……地方
> move in 搬进
> move out 搬出来
> move away 搬走
> move into 搬进（由外到内的过程）

We're going to _____ next week.

3. **miss** *v.* 想念，思念

> miss *v.* 想念，思念
> have in mind 思念，想到，考虑到，记得

I'm sure that everybody will _____ him very much.

4. **neighbour** *n.* 邻居

> neighbour　*n.* 邻居
> neighbourliness　*n.* 亲切，友善，和睦
> neighbourhood　*n.* 邻居关系，邻接，附近邻里情谊
> neighbouring　*adj.* 附近的，毗邻的
> neighbourly　*adj.* 像邻居的，亲切的，和睦的
> neighbourship　*n.* 邻居关系

Canada and the United States are _____.

5. **person**　*n.* 人

> person　*n.* 人
> person insuring　保险人
> person to person　叫人电话
> person-to-person　*adj.* 人与人之间直接的，（长途电话）指定受话人的

We need a _____ to help us.

6. **people**　*n.* 人们

> people　*n.* 人们
> people journalism　名人新闻报道
> peoplehood　*n.* 民族性，民族意识
> peopleless　*adj.* 无人的，无人居住的

Were there many _____ at the party?

7. **poor**　*adj.* 可怜的

> poor　*adj.* 可怜的
> poor as a church　一贫如洗
> poor box　慈善箱，捐款箱
> poor crop　欠收
> poor farm　救济农场

We couldn't rescue the _____ fellow.

II Make sentences using the under-mentioned words 单词造句

still — miss

_____.

move — tired

_____.

neighbour — person

_____.

people — poor

_____.

III Match 连线

- individual human being   still
- human beings   move
- person living in a house, street, etc. near another   miss
- deserving or causing pity   neighbour
- notice or regret the absence   person
- change one's place of living   people
- up to now   poor

IV Glossary 词汇表

still　*adv.*　还，仍旧
move　*v.*　搬家
miss　*v.*　想念，思念
neighbour　*n.*　邻居
person　*n.*　人
people　*n.*　人们
poor　*adj.*　可怜的

Lesson 80

Our new neighbour
我们的新邻居

I New words 新单词

1. **pilot** *n.* 飞行员

> pilot *n.* 飞行员
> pilot chart 引航图
> pilot lamp 指示灯
> pilot light 信号灯，指示灯，领航灯

The _____ landed the plane safely.

2. **return** *v.* 返回

> return *v.* 返回
> return address 回寄地址，寄件人地址
> return fare 来回路费，往返票价
> return of goods 退货

He's just _____ from abroad.

3. **New York** *n.* 纽约

> New York *n.* 纽约
> New York City 纽约市
> New Yorker 纽约州人或居民

Have you ever been to _____ city?

4. **Tokyo** *n.* 东京

   _____ is the capital of Japan.

5. **Madrid** *n.* 马德里

   They'll take an evening flight to _____.

6. **fly**（**flew/flown**） *v.* 飞行

   > fly（flew/flown） *v.* 飞行
   > fly a kite   放风筝，试探舆论
   > fly about   翱翔，（消息，思想等）四下飞速传播
   > fly around   急速地走来走去

   Clouds were _____ across the sky.

II Make sentences using the under-mentioned words 单词造句

pilot — New York

_____.

return — Madrid

_____.

Tokyo — fly

_____.

III Match 连线

- move through the air with wings   pilot
- the capital of Spain   return
- the capital of Japan   New York
- a person who flies an airplane   Tokyo
- coming or going back to a place   Madrid
- a city of America   fly（flew/flown）

Ⅳ Glossary 词汇表

pilot   *n.* 飞行员
return   *v.* 返回
New York   *n.* 纽约
Tokyo   *n.* 东京
Madrid   *n.* 马德里
fly（flew/flown）   *v.* 飞行

Lesson 81

When did you/will you go to...?

你过去/将在什么时候去……?

I New words 新单词

1. **Athens**   *n.* 雅典

> Athens   *n.* 雅典
> Athena   *n.* 雅典娜（智慧，技艺，学问，战争女神）
> Athenian   *n.* 雅典人

Modern Olympic Games origins from _____.

2. **Berlin**   *n.* 柏林

They attended the last _____ International Film Festival.

3. **Bombay**   *n.* 孟买

We flew from London to _____ in one hop.

4. **Geneva**   *n.* 日内瓦

> Geneva   *n.* 日内瓦
> Genevan   *adj.* 日内瓦的

I'll pay a visit to one of my friends in _____.

5. **Moscow**   *n.* 莫斯科

> Moscow   *n.* 莫斯科
> Muscovite   *adj.* 莫斯科的，俄国的；*n.* 俄国人

_____ is a very beautiful city.

6. **Rome** *n.* 罗马

> Rome   *n.* 罗马
> Roman   *n.* 罗马人的，罗马的
> Roman nose   高鼻梁鼻子，鹰钩鼻
> Roman numerals   罗马数字

When in _____ , do as the Romans do.

7. **Seoul** *n.* 首尔

_____ is the capital and largest city of South Korea.

8. **Stockholm** *n.* 斯德哥尔摩

He's studying art at _____ University.

9. **Sydney** *n.* 悉尼

Who designed the _____ Opera House?

II Make sentences using the under-mentioned words 单词造句

Athens — beautiful
_____.

Berlin — Germany
_____.

Bombay — Indian
_____.

Geneva — meeting
_____.

Moscow — Russia
_____.

Rome — church
_____.

Seoul — Korea

_____.

Stockholm — Sweden

_____.

Sydney — Australia

_____.

Ⅲ Match 连线

- a famous city of Australia
- the capital of Sweden
- the capital of Korea
- the capital of Russia
- a country in Europe
- the capital of Greece
- the capital of Germany
- a city in the southeast of Switzerland
- an area in the west part of India

Athens
Berlin
Bombay
Geneva
Moscow
Rome
Seoul
Stockholm
Sydney

Ⅳ Glossary 词汇表

Athens   *n.* 雅典
Berlin   *n.* 柏林
Bombay   *n.* 孟买
Geneva   *n.* 日内瓦
Moscow   *n.* 莫斯科
Rome   *n.* 罗马
Seoul   *n.* 首尔
Stockholm   *n.* 斯德哥尔摩
Sydney   *n.* 悉尼

Lesson 82

Tickets, please.
请把车票拿出来。

I New words 新单词

1. **return** *n.* 往返

> return *n.* 往返
> return ticket 往返车票
> return fare 来回路费
> return freight 往返运费

On my _____ from work, I saw the door was open.

2. **train** *n.* 火车

> train *n.* 火车
> by train 乘火车
> train dispatch 列车调度员
> train sickness 晕车

Are you travelling by _____?

3. **platform** *n.* 站台

> platform *n.* 站台
> platform balance 台秤
> platform bridge 天桥

The train at _____ 2 goes to the city.

4. **plenty** *n.* 大量

> plenty *n.* 大量
> plenty of + 可数或不可数名词 大量的，多的
> a great deal 大量，许多

Drink _____ of water in Spring.

5. **bar** *n.* 酒吧

> bar *n.* 酒吧
> a/the bar for singles 单身酒吧

Is this the _____ for singles?

6. **station** *n.* 车站，火车站

> station *n.* 车站，火车站
> railway station 火车站
> bus station/stop 公共汽车站

Which _____ are you going to?

7. **porter** *n.* 乘务员

> porter *n.* 乘务员
> porterage *n.* 运输业，运费
> check taker 收票员

He tried to slip past the _____.

8. **catch**（**caught/caught**） *v.* 赶上

> catch（caught/caught） *v.* 赶上
> catch a bus 赶公共汽车
> catch a cold 感冒
> catch up with 赶上，逮捕，处罚

Every morning she would _____ the 7:30 train to town.

9. **miss** *v.* 错过

> miss *v.* 错过
> miss out 遗漏
> miss the boat 错失良机

I was late because I _____ the bus.

II Make sentences using the under-mentioned words 单词造句

return — train

_____.

platform — station

_____.

plenty — bar

_____.

porter — ticket

_____.

catch — miss

_____.

III Match 连线

- fail to catch   return
- be in time for sth.   train
- person employed to carry traveler's luggage   platform
- stopping place along a transportation route   plenty
- come or go back to a place   bar
- a place where people can buy and have drinks and   station
  sometimes food
- carriages or wagons that are pulled by an engine   porter
  along a railway line

- the part of a railway station where you stand to   catch
  wait for a train
- a great deal   miss

Ⅳ Glossary 词汇表

return   *n.* 往返
train   *n.* 火车
platform   *n.* 站台
plenty   *n.* 大量
bar   *n.* 酒吧
station   *n.* 车站, 火车站
porter   *n.* 乘务员
catch （caught/caught）   *v.* 赶上
miss   *v.* 错过

Lesson
83

A small blue case
一只蓝色的小箱子

I New words 新单词 ....

1. leave（left/left） *v.* 遗留

> leave（left/left） *v.* 遗留
> leave a message 留话
> leave alone 不管
> leave behind 遗落，丢下，放弃

She _____ a young son after her death.

2. describe *v.* 描述

> describe *v.* 描述
> description *n.* 描述，描绘，说明
> descriptive *adj.* 描述的，记述的

She _____ the woman to the police.

3. zip *n.* 拉链

> zip *n.* 拉链
> zip-out *adj.* 用拉链系合的
> zip up 扣上或拉上（拉链）
> zipper *n.* 使用拉链的人，装上拉链的物件

The _____ is stuck.

4. label *n.* 标签

> label   *n.* 标签
> labeled   *adj.* 加有标记的

Attractive _____ is very necessary.

5. **handle**   *n.* 提手，把手

> handle   *n.* 提手，把手
> handlebar   *n.* （自行车等的）把手

He turned the _____ and opened the door.

6. **address**   *n.* 地址

> address   *n.* 地址
> address book   通信录
> address field   地址栏
> addressable   *adj.* 可编址的，可寻址的

Could you please let me know your e-mail _____?

7. **pence**   *n.* 便士（penny 的复数形式）

She had no _____ in her pocket.

8. **belong**   *v.* 属于

> belong   *v.* 属于
> belong to   属于
> belonging   *n.* 所有物，附属品，归属，财产

Does this book _____ to you?

II *Make sentences using the under-mentioned words* 单词造句

leave — address

_____.

describe — label

_____.

zip — bag

_____.

handle — door

_____.

pence — belong

_____.

Ⅲ Match 连线

- be owned by person or group
- the plural form of penny
- the number of the house and the name of the street and town where one lives and work
- the part of a thing that you hold in your hand
- not bring something with you
- say what sb. or sth. is like or what happened
- a long metal or plastic thing with a small part that you pull to close and open things
- a piece of paper plastic on something that tells you about it

leave（left/left）

describe

zip

label

handle

address

pence

belong

Ⅳ Glossary 词汇表

leave（left/left）　*v.* 遗留
describe　*v.* 描述
zip　*n.* 拉链
label　*n.* 标签
handle　*n.* 提手，把手
address　*n.* 地址
pence　*n.* 便士（penny 的复数形式）
belong　*v.* 属于

Lesson
84

Ow!

啊哟！

I New words 新单词

1. ow *int.* 啊哟

> ow *int.* 啊哟
> whoops *int.* (表示惊讶，困窘或道歉之感叹词)哎哟
> ouch *int.* 哎哟

_____ ! My tooth is killing me!

2. slip *v.* 滑倒

> slip *v.* 滑倒
> slippery *adj.* 光滑的
> slip noose 滑结套，活结套

The soap _____ out of her hand.

3. fall（**fell/fallen**） *v.* 落下，跌倒

> fall（fell/fallen） *v.* 落下，跌倒
> fall behind 落后
> fall down 掉下，跌倒

Leaves begin to _____ in October.

4. downstairs *adv.* 下楼

> downstairs *adv.* 下楼
> upstairs *adv.* 上楼

He went _____ to answer the front door.

5. **hurt** (hurt/hurt) *v.* 伤，伤害，疼痛

> hurt （hurt/hurt） *v.* 伤，伤害，疼痛
> hurtful *adj.* 引起疼痛的，伤感情的

I don't mean to _____ you.

6. **back** *n.* 背

> back *n.* 背
> back to back 背靠背，一个接一个
> backache *n.* 背痛

She put the saddle on the horse's _____.

7. **stand up** 起立，站起来

> stand up 起立，站起来
> stand about 闲散地站着
> stand aside 站开，让开，退出
> stand by 站在旁边，袖手旁观，支持，忠于

_____, please.

8. **help** *v.* 帮助

> help *v.* 帮助
> help sb. do sth. /help sb. to do sth. 帮助某人做
> 　某事
> help each other 彼此帮助

He devoted his life to _____ the disabled.

9. **at once** 立即

> at once 立即
> immediately *adv.* 立即，马上
> promptly *adv.* 迅速地，敏捷地

Do it _____ !

10. **sure**　*adj.* 一定的，确信的

> sure　*adj.* 一定的，确信的
> surely　*adv.* 确实，当然，无疑
> sureness　*n.* 真确，踏实
> certain　*adj.* 一定的，确实的

I am _____ that I put the money in the box.

11. **X-ray**　*n.* X 光透视

> X-ray　*n.* X 光透视
> X-ray photograph　X 射线照片，X 光照片
> X-ray therapy　X 光治疗法
> X radiation　X 射线，X 辐射

It would be better for you to have an _____ .

II Make sentences using the under-mentioned words 单词造句

ow — slip

_____ .

fall — downstairs

_____ .

hurt — back

_____ .

stand up — help

_____ .

at once — X-ray

_____ .

sure — thing

_____ .

III Match 连线

- rays used in treatment of diseases   ow
- reliable or without doubt   slip
- immediately   fall（fell/fallen）
- give aid or relief to   downstairs
- the part of a person or an animal between   hurt（hurt/hurt）
  the neck and the bottom
- get up on your feet   back
- slide suddenly   stand up
- you say "ow" when you suddenly feel pain   help
- drop；go down quickly   at once
- to a lower a floor of a building   sure
- make somebody feel pain   X-ray

IV Glossary 词汇表

ow   *int.* 啊哟

slip   *v.* 滑倒

fall（fell/fallen） *v.* 落下，跌倒

downstairs   *adv.* 下楼

hurt（hurt/hurt） *v.* 伤，伤害，疼痛

back   *n.* 背

stand up   起立，站起来

help   *v.* 帮助

at once   立即

sure   *adj.* 一定的，确信的

X-ray   *n.* X 光透视

85

He says that...
She says that...
They say that...
他/她/他们说……

I New words 新单词

1. **licence** *n.* 执照

> licence *n.* 执照
> a driver's/driving licence　驾驶执照
> a dog licence　狗牌照
> grant/issue a licence　颁发执照
> revoke a licence　吊销执照
> suspend a licence　暂时吊销执照

The policeman asked to see his driving _____.

II Make sentences using the under-mentioned words 单词造句

licence — car

_____.

III Match 连线

- written or printed statement giving perssion from　　licence
  someone in authority for sb. to do sth.

IV *Glossary* 词汇表

licence   *n.* 执照

A card from Jimmy
吉米的明信片

Ⅰ New words 新单词

1. **Scotland** *n.* 苏格兰（英国）

> Scotland *n.* 苏格兰（英国）
> Scottish *adj.* 苏格兰的，苏格兰人的

_____ borders England.

2. **card** *n.* 明信片

> card *n.* 明信片
> have the cards in one's hands 有成功的把握
> play one's trump cards 打出王牌
> show one's cards 摊牌

I sent several Christmas _____ to my friends.

3. **youth** *n.* 青年

> youth *n.* 青年
> young *adj.* 年轻的
> youth club 青年俱乐部
> youth hostel 青年招待所

In his _____ he was a soldier.

4. **hostel** *n.* 招待所，旅馆

> hostel   *n.* 招待所，旅馆
> hosteler   *n.* 青年旅行者，旅店老板
> hostelry   *n.* 旅馆，客栈

I lived in a _____ while I was a student.

5. **association**   *n.* 协会

> association   *n.* 协会
> the Youth Hostels Association（the Y. H. A.）青
>   年招待所协会，简称"青招协"

Do you belong to any professional _____?

6. **soon**   *adv.* 不久

> soon   *adv.* 不久
> as soon as   一……就
> the sooner the better   越快越好
> sooner or later   迟早

_____ she would have to resign.

7. **write**（**wrote/written**）*v.* 写

> write（wrote/written）*v.* 写
> write back   回信
> writable   *adj.* 可写下的，能写成文的
> write down   写下，记下

I'll _____ to you soon.

II *Make sentences using the under-mentioned words* 单词造句

Scotland — Britain

_____

card — write

_____.

youth — hostel

_____.

association — soon

_____.

III Match 连线

- a part of Britain where its people speak Scottish   card
- state or period when one is still young   Scotland
- a lodging-house for students or other special group   youth
- producing symbols, usually letters, on a surface   hostel
- within a short time   association
- associating, organized body of people with   soon
  the same interests
- piece of stiff paper or cardboard used for   write (wrote/
  various purposes   written)

IV Glossary 词汇表

Scotland   *n.* 苏格兰（英国）
card   *n.* 明信片
youth   *n.* 青年
hostel   *n.* 招待所，旅馆
association   *n.* 协会
soon   *adv.* 不久
write（wrote/written） *v.* 写

Lesson 87

The French test
法语考试

I New words 新单词

1. **exam** *n.* 考试

> exam　*n.* 考试
> midterm exam　期中考试
> final exam　期末考试
> entrance examination　入学考试
> sham exam　模拟考试

Did you pass your chemistry _____?

2. **pass** *v.* 及格，通过

> pass　*v.* 及格，通过
> pass by　经过，掠过
> pass down　遗传
> pass mark　及格分数
> pass the exam　通过某一个考试
> pass in + 具体的科目　通过某一科目的考试

I think I _____ the exam.

3. **mathematics** *n.* （maths 是缩写）数学

> mathematics　*n.* （maths 是缩写）数学
> mathematic　*adj.* 数学的，精确的无疑的
> mathematician　*n.* 数学家，善做数字计算的人

He is good at _____.

4. **question**   *n.* （具体的某一个）问题

> question   *n.* （具体的某一个）问题
> question mark   问号，难题
> question of fact   事实问题
> questionable   *adj.* 可疑的，不肯定的，靠不住的

You haven't answered my _____.

5. **easy**   *adj.* 容易的

> easy   *adj.* 容易的
> easy as my eye   易如反掌
> easy chair   安乐椅，安乐处境，恬适
> easy circumstances   富裕，安逸生活

It was an _____ job and we did it quickly.

6. **enough**   *adv.* 足够地

> enough   *adv.* 足够地
> enough and to spare   足够而且绰绰有余
> enough is as good as a feast   饱餐不比筵席差

Is the fish cooked _____?

7. **paper**   *n.* 考卷

> paper   *n.* 考卷
> paper boy   卖报童，送报童
> paper clip   纸夹，回文针
> the English and Maths papers   英文和数学卷子

She looked at the examination _____ with a frown.

8. **fail**   *v.* 未及格，失败

> fail *v.* 未及格，失败
> fail in 在……上失败，变弱
> fail of 不能获得（成功等），不履行（职责等），缺乏
> failed *adj.* 失败了的

Doctors _____ to save the old man's life.

9. **answer** *v.* 回答

> answer *v.* 回答
> answer back 顶嘴，回应
> answer sheet 答案纸
> answer the door 应门，去开门（迎客）
> answerer *n.* 回答者，解答者，答辩者

Who can _____ the question?

10. **mark** *n.* 分数

> mark *n.* 分数
> mark down 降低给（班级，学生）的分数，记录
> mark on 标上

The teacher gave me a good _____ for my composition.

11. **rest** *n.* 其他的东西

> rest *n.* 其他的东西
> else *adj.* 另外的，其他的
> other *adj.* 其他的，其余得，另外的，从前的

The beginning was boring, but the _____ was interesting.

12. **difficult** *adj.* 困难的

> difficult *adj.* 困难的
> difficulty *n.* 困难性，困难程度，麻烦

Nothing is _____ to a man who wills.

13. **hate** *v.* 讨厌

> hate   *v.* 讨厌
> hateable   *adj.* 可憎恨的，该遭憎恨的
> hateful   *adj.* 讨厌的，可恶的

The kindhearted people _____ violence.

14. **low** *adj.* 低的

> low   *adj.* 低的
> low-cost   *adj.* 成本低的，代价小的
> low-fat   *adj.* 低脂肪的
> low-grade   *adj.* 质量差的，低等的

The temperature was very _____ this early morning.

15. **cheer** *v.* 振作，振奋

> cheer   *v.* 振作，振奋
> cheer up   振作起来
> cheer on   鼓励
> cheering   *adj.* 令人振奋的

The crowd _____ as the teams entered the field.

16. **guy** *n.* 家伙，人

> guy   *n.* 家伙，人
> fellow   *n.* 家伙，小伙子

He's a tough _____.

17. **top** *n.* 上方，顶部

> top   *n.* 上方，顶部
> at the top of   在……顶端

> at the bottom of   在……末（底）端
> top-level   *adj.* 最高级的

He climbed to the _____ of the hill.

II Make sentences using the under-mentioned words 单词造句

exam — pass

_____.

mathematics — fail

_____.

question — answer

_____.

easy — enough

_____.

paper — mark

_____.

rest — hate

_____.

difficult — cheer

_____.

low — top

_____.

guy — strong

_____.

III Match 连线

- a request for information   exam
- science of numbers, quantity and space   pass
- examination   mathematics

- success in an examination
- a poor academic grade; be unsuccessful
- a group of questions in an examination
- not difficult
- as much or as many as you need
- not easy to do or understand
- the other people or thing
- say or write something when somebody has asked a question
- a number or letter that a teacher gives for your work to show how good it is
- a man; person
- fill with gladness, hope, high spirits
- have a strong feeling of not liking somebody or something
- the highest part of something
- not high; near the ground

question
easy
enough
paper
fail
answer
mark
rest

difficult

hate
low
cheer

guy
top

Ⅳ Glossary 词汇表

exam　*n.* 考试

pass　*v.* 及格, 通过

mathematics　*n.* (maths 是缩写) 数学

question　*n.* (具体的某一个) 问题

easy　*adj.* 容易的

enough　*adv.* 足够地

paper　*n.* 考卷

fail　*v.* 未及格, 失败

answer　*v.* 回答

mark　*n.* 分数

rest　*n.* 其他的东西

difficult *adj.* 困难的
hate *v.* 讨厌
low *adj.* 低的
cheer *v.* 振作，振奋
guy *n.* 家伙，人
top *n.* 上方，顶部

Too, very, enough
太、非常、足够

Ⅰ New words 新单词 ....

1. clever *adj.* 聪明的

> clever   *adj.* 聪明的
> bright   伶俐的
> intelligent   智商高
> smart   聪明的
> shrewd   精明的
> wise   博学的，明智的
> gifted   有天赋的
> talented   聪明的，通过能力获得的才能

He is not _____ but hard-working.

2. stupid *adj.* 笨的

> stupid   *adj.* 笨的
> stupidity   *n.* 愚蠢，笨，呆头呆脑
> stupidly   *adv.* 笨的，愚蠢的，麻木的

Do not be _____ !

3. cheap *adj.* 便宜的

> cheap   *adj.* 便宜的
> cheapen   *v.* 减价，降价

cheaply　*adj.* 便宜的，不值钱的
cheapness　*n.* 便宜，廉价

Fresh vegetables are very _____ in the summer.

4. **expensive** *adj.* 贵的

expensive　*adj.* 贵的
expensively　*adj.* 昂贵的，花钱大手大脚的
dear　*adj.* 昂贵的，贵重的，宝贵的

It is _____ to travel by plane.

5. **fresh** *adj.* 新鲜的

fresh　*adj.* 新鲜的
fresh arrival　新到货
fresh supply　新的供应
freshen　*v.* 变得新鲜

This fish isn't _____, it smells!

6. **stale** *adj.* 不新鲜的，变味的

stale　*adj.* 不新鲜的，变味的
stale check　过期支票
stale market　呆滞的市场
staleness　*n.* 腐坏，腐烂，泄气

Flowing water does not get _____.

7. **low** *adj.* 低的，矮的

low　*adj.* 低的，矮的
low area　低气压区
low comedy　低级喜剧，滑稽戏
low-lying　*adj.* 地势低洼的

You must use a _____ gear to drive up the hill.

8. **loud** *adj.* 大声的

> loud *adj.* 大声的
> loud-spoken *adj.* 高声说话的，嗓门大的
> louden *v.* 使响亮
> loudish *adj.* 相当响亮的

The teacher's voice is very _____ ; we can all hear it.

9. **high** *adj.* 高的

> high *adj.* 高的
> high and mighty 显赫人物，神气活现者
> high blood pressure 高血压
> high-blooded *adj.* 出身高贵的，血统纯正的

The bird sang _____ and clearly in the tree.

10. **hard** *adj.* 硬的

> hard *adj.* 硬的
> hard-and-fast *adj.* 坚定的，不变动的
> hard-boiled *adj.* 强硬的，不动感情的，（蛋）煮的老的
> hard cash 硬币，现金

The snow has frozen _____ on the road.

11. **sweet** *adj.* 甜的

> sweet *adj.* 甜的
> sweet oil 芳香的食用油
> sweet pea 香豌豆
> sweet potato 红薯，甘薯
> sweet shop 糖果店
> sweet talk 甜言蜜语

You shouldn't eat so much _____ stuff.

12. **soft** *adj.* 软的

> soft *adj.* 软的
> soft currency 软通货
> soft drink 软饮料（不含酒精的充碳酸性饮料），汽水
> soft landing 软着陆
> soften *v.* 变软，软化，使缓和

Cotton feels _____.

13. **sour** *adj.* 酸的

> sour *adj.* 酸的
> sour grapes 酸葡萄
> sourball *n.* 酸味水果硬糖，脾气暴躁的人

The fruit was too _____to eat.

Ⅱ *Make sentences using the under-mentioned words* 单词造句

clever — stupid
_____.

cheap — soft
_____.

expensive — hard
_____.

fresh — stale
_____.

low — high
_____.

loud — voice
_____.

sweet — sour
_____.

III Match 连线

- causing expense, high priced
- low in price; worth more in the cost
- quick in learning and understanding; skillful
- not clever and intelligent
- easily heard; noisy, not quiet or soft
- below the usual lever
- newly made or produced
- not fresh
- tasting as if it contains sugar
- far above ground or sea level
- having an extremely acid taste
- not hard or firm
- not soft; solid and firm

clever
stupid
cheap
expensive
fresh
stale
low
loud
high
hard
sweet
soft
sour

IV Glossary 词汇表

clever　*adj.*　聪明的

stupid　*adj.*　笨的

cheap　*adj.*　便宜的

expensive　*adj.*　贵的

fresh　*adj.*　新鲜的

stale　*adj.*　不新鲜的，变味的

low　*adj.*　低的，矮的

loud　*adj.*　大声的

high　*adj.*　高的

hard　*adj.*　硬的

sweet　*adj.*　甜的

soft　*adj.*　软的

sour　*adj.*　酸的

Full of mistakes
错误百出

I New words 新单词

1. **spell** (spelt/spelt) v. 拼写

> spell (spelt/spelt) v. 拼写
> spell out 把（词的）字母拼写出，讲清楚
> spelldown n. 拼单词比赛
> speller n. 拼单词者，单词拼写课本
> spelling n. 拼写，拼读

Can you _____ your name?

2. **intelligent** adj. 聪明的，有智慧的

> intelligent adj. 聪明的，有智慧的
> intelligence n. 智慧，聪颖，悟性
> bright adj. 聪明的，明亮的，清澈的
> clever adj. 聪明的，精明的，灵巧的

Are dolphins more _____ than other animals?

3. **mistake** n. 错误

> mistake n. 错误
> make a mistake 出错
> mistakeable adj. 易出错的，易误解的
> mistake A for B 把 A 误认为 B
> mistaken adj. 犯错的，错误的，误会的

She always makes some _____ in the homework.

4. **present**　*n.* 礼物

> present　*n.* 礼物
> presentation　*n.* 礼物，赠送，授予，描述
> presentee　*n.* 受赠者
> presenter　*n.* 赠送者，呈献者，提出者
> gift　*n.* 礼物

He unwrapped his Christmas _____ with delight.

5. **dictionary**　*n.* 词典

> dictionary　*n.* 词典
> lexicon　*n.* 词典，字典，专门词汇
> lexicography　*n.* 词典编撰，词典编撰学

Whose _____ is this?

Ⅱ *Make sentences using the under-mentioned words* 单词造句

spell — mistake

_____.

intelligent — boy

_____.

present — dictionary

_____.

Ⅲ Match 连线

- wrong idea or opinion; thing done　　　spell（spelt/spelt）
  incorrectly
- gift　　　　　　　　　　　　　　　　intelligent

- a book that gives words from A to Z and explains what each word means   mistake
- use the right letters to make a word   present
- clever; bright   dictionary

IV Glossary 词汇表

spell (spelt/spelt) *v.* 拼写

intelligent *adj.* 聪明的，有智慧的

mistake *n.* 错误

present *n.* 礼物

dictionary *n.* 词典

Lesson 90

I want you / him / her / them to...

我要你 / 他 / 她 / 他们……

Tell him / her / them to...

告诉他 / 她 / 他们……

I New words 新单词

1. **carry** *v.* 带

> carry *v.* 带
> carry away 搬去，使失去自制力
> carry back 运回，使……回想
> carry-home *adj.* 便于携带的
> take *v.* 取，拿，带走，拿走

These bags _____ easily.

2. **keep** *v.* 保存，保留

> keep *v.* 保存，保留
> keep a record 作记录
> keep abreast of 保持与……并驾齐驱
> keep an eye on 留意，照料
> keep fit 保持健康，保持体形

I'll _____ the original copy of your report on file.

3. **correct** *v.* 改正，纠正

> correct　*v.* 改正，纠正
> correction　*n.* 改正，校正，修正
> correction fluid　修正液
> correctional　*adj.* 改正的，修正的

I spent the whole morning _____ exam papers.

II Make sentences using the under-mentioned words 单词造句

carry — bag

_____.

correct — keep

_____.

III Match 连线

- to set right; to remove errors　　　　　　carry
- put aside for a future time　　　　　　　correct
- hold something; take　　　　　　　　　　keep

IV Glossary 词汇表

> carry　*v.* 带
> keep　*v.* 保存，保留
> correct　*v.* 改正，纠正

Lesson 91

It's so small.

太小了。

1. **madam** *n.* 夫人，女士（对妇女的尊称）

> madam *n.* 夫人，女士（对妇女的尊称）
> lady *n.* 夫人，女士，小姐，贵族夫人（小姐）

Can I help you, _____?

2. **smart** *adj.* 漂亮的

> smart *adj.* 漂亮的
> smarted up 装扮的很漂亮的
> smarten *v.* 打扮，修饰

She always wears _____ clothes.

3. **as well** 同样

> as well 同样
> as well as 与……相同，此外，也
> same *adj.* 相同的，同样的

I can do it _____.

4. **suit** *v.* 适于

> suit *v.* 适于
> suitable *adj.* 合适的，适宜的，适用的
> suitably *adv.* 合宜地，适当地
> suitability *n.* 适当，适宜，相配

One o'clock does not _____ me.

5. **pretty**   *adj.* 漂亮的

> pretty   *adj.* 漂亮的
> prettyish   *adj.* 有点可爱的，相当美的
> beautiful   *adj.* 漂亮的
> good-looking   *adj.* 好看的，漂亮的

Susan is a _____ girl.

II Make sentences using the under-mentioned words 单词造句

madam — pretty

_____.

smart — as well

_____.

suit — age

_____.

III Match 连线

- beautiful   madam
- same   smart
- meet the requirements of   as well
- lady   suit
- active; stylish   pretty

IV Glossary 词汇表

> madam   *n.* 夫人，女士（对妇女的尊称）
> smart   *adj.* 漂亮的
> as well   同样
> suit   *v.* 适于
> pretty   *adj.* 漂亮的

Lesson

92

A good idea

好主意

I New words 新单词

1. **idea** *n.* 主意

> idea *n.* 主意
> good idea 好主意
> opinion 对某事具体的看法、观点、想法

She'll have her own _____ about that.

2. **a little** 少许（用于不可数名词之前）

> a little 少许（用于不可数名词之前）
> little 少许（用于不可数名词之前）

I felt _____ better.

3. **teaspoonful** *adj.* 一满茶匙的

> teaspoonful *adj.* 一满茶匙的
> teaspoon *n.* 茶匙

Put a _____ of salt into the pan.

4. **less** *adj.*（little 的比较级）较少的，更小的

> less *adj.*（little 的比较级）较少的，更小的
> less than 少于……，……更少的

She received _____ than she asked for.

5. **a few** 几个（用于可数名词之前）

> a few 几个（用于可数名词之前）
> few 几个（用于可数名词之前）

She will arrive in _____ minutes.

6. **pity** *n.* 遗憾

> pity *n.* 遗憾
> regret *n.* 后悔

It's a _____ that you have to go so soon.

7. **instead** *adv.* 代替

> instead *adv.* 代替
> intead of 代替
> replace *v.* 代替，取代，替换

I'm tired and can't attend the meeting; you could go _____.

8. **advice** *n.* 建议，忠告

> advice *n.* 建议，忠告
> advise *v.* 建议，忠告，劝告
> a piece of advice 一条建议
> take one's advice 听从某人的建议
> follow one's advice 采纳某人的建议

You'd better take my _____ next time.

II *Make sentences using the under-mentioned words* 单词造句

idea — advice

_____.

a little — pity

_____.

teaspoonful — instead

_____ .

less — than

_____ .

a few — people

_____ .

Ⅲ Match 连线

- not so much; a smaller amount of something
- a teaspoon filled with something
- opinion
- some but not much
- words that you say to help sb. to decide what to do
- replace; in the place of sb. or sth.
- some but not many
- feeling of sorrow for another person's suffering

idea

a little

teaspoonful

less

a few

pity

instead

advice

Ⅳ Glossary 词汇表

idea　*n.* 主意

a little　少许（用于不可数名词之前）

teaspoonful　*adj.* 一满茶匙的

less　*adj.*（little 的比较级）较少的，更小的

a few　几个（用于可数名词之前）

pity　*n.* 遗憾

instead　*adv.* 代替

advice　*n.* 建议，忠告

Lesson 93

How do they compare? 比一比

I New words 新单词

1. **most** （many, much 的最高级） *adj.* 最多的

> most（many, much 的最高级） *adj.* 最多的
> mostly *adv.* 多半，几乎全部地，通常
> majority *adj.* 多数的，过半数的

She has the _____ to gain.

2. **least** （little 的最高级） *adj.* 最小的，最少的

> least（little 的最高级） *adj.* 最小的，最少的
> at least 最低限度，至少
> least possible value 最小可能的值
> minimum *adj.* 最少的，最低的

The _____ you can do is to be polite.

3. **best** （good 的最高级） *adj.* 最好的

> best（good 的最高级） *adj.* 最好的
> best bid 最高出价
> best in quality 品质优良
> best of all 尤其，首先，最
> best price 最优价格

Strive for the _____, prepare for the worst.

4. **worse**（bad 的比较级）   *adj.* 更坏的

> worse（bad 的比较级）   *adj.* 更坏的
> worse and worse   越来越坏，每况愈下
> worse luck   更不幸地
> worsen   *v.* 变得更坏，使恶化

He's getting steadily _____.

5. **worst**（bad 的最高级）   *adj.* 最坏的

> worst（bad 的最高级）   *adj.* 最坏的
> worst-case   *adj.* 做最坏打算的，为最坏情况的

It's the _____ dinner I ever ate.

Ⅱ Make sentences using the under-mentioned words 单词造句

most — least

_____.

best — worst

_____.

worse — condition

_____.

Ⅲ Match 连线

- most good/well   most
- less good   least
- most bad   best
- the biggest amount or number of something   worse
- the smallest amount of something   worst

Ⅳ Glossary 词汇表

most（many, much 的最高级） *adj.* 最多的
least（little 的最高级） *adj.* 最小的，最少的
best（good 的最高级） *adj.* 最好的
worse（bad 的比较级） *adj.* 更坏的
worst（bad 的最高级） *adj.* 最坏的

Lesson

94 The most expensive model
最昂贵的型号

I New words 新单词

1. **model** *n.* 型号，式样

> model *n.* 型号，式样
> model contract 合同样本
> modeler *n.* 制造模型者
> modeling *adj.* 模特的，造型的；*n.* 造型，塑性

The car industry's always producing new _____ .

2. **afford** *v.* 付得起（钱）

> afford *v.* 付得起（钱）
> affordable *adj.* 供应得起的，可提供的，可给予的

We can't _____ such enormous fees.

3. **deposit** *n.* 预付定金

> deposit *n.* 预付定金
> deposit for security 保证金
> deposit premium 预付保险费
> pay a deposit of 付……钱定金

He put down a _____ on the house yesterday.

4. **instalment** *n.* 分期付款

> instalment *n.* 分期付款
> buy sth. on instalments 分期付款买……

I want to buy a house on _____ this year.

5. **price** *n.* 价格

> price *n.* 价格
> price analysis 价格分析
> price association 价格联盟
> price bargain 讨价还价
> price boom 价格暴涨

The _____ of that house is high.

6. **millionaire** *n.* 百万富翁

> millionaire *n.* 百万富翁
> million *n.* 百万; *adj.* 百万的
> millionaires *n.* 女百万富翁, 百万富翁的妻子

His father is a self-made _____.

Ⅱ *Make sentences using the under-mentioned words* 单词造句

model — price

_____.

afford — millionaire

_____.

deposit — instalment

_____.

Ⅲ Match 连线

- a part of the cost of something that you pay   model
  each week or month, for example
- a very rich person who has more than a million   afford
  pounds, dollars, etc.

- amount of money for which something is sold or bought　　　　　deposit
- design or size of something　　　　　instalment
- money that you pay to show that you want something and that you will pay the rest later　　　　　price
- have enough money to pay for something　　　　　millionaire

IV Glossary 词汇表

> model　　*n.*　型号，式样
> afford　　*v.*　付得起（钱）
> deposit　　*n.*　预付定金
> instalment　　*n.*　分期付款
> price　　*n.*　价格
> millionaire　　*n.*　百万富翁

Small change

零钱

I New words 新单词

1. **conductor** *n.* 售票员

> conductor *n.* 售票员
> conductress *n.* 女售票员，女列车长，女指挥
> conduct *v.* 任售票员，引导，指挥

The _____ handed the stickman out of the bus.

2. **fare** *n.* 车费，车票

> fare *n.* 车费，车票
> fare box *n.* （公共汽车等的）废票箱
> farer *n.* 旅行者

She didn't have enough money for the bus _____.

3. **change** *v.* 兑换（钱）

> change *v.* 兑换（钱）
> exchange *v.* 兑换，交换；*n.* 外汇，汇价，
> 票据

I want to _____ the pounds into dollars.

4. **note** *n.* 纸币

> note *n.* 纸币
> paper money 纸币

> cash　*n.* 小铜钱，现金
> note in circulation　流通中的货币

Her mother gave her a pound _____ .

5. **passenger**　*n.* 乘客

> passenger　*n.* 乘客
> passenger train　客车
> goods train　货车
> passenger liner　定期客船，客运班机
> passenger list（班机或班轮用的）旅客名单

This is a _____ train, not a goods train.

6. **none**　*pron.* 没有任何东西

> none　*pron.* 没有任何东西
> one but　除……之外没有，只有
> none other than　不是别人而正是
> no　*adj.* 没有的（形容词，在句中一般修饰别
> 　的名词）

I bought _____ .

7. **neither**　*adv.* 也不

> neither　*adv.* 也不
> nor　*conj.* ……也不，……也没有

He doesn't smoke, _____ does he drink.

8. **get off**　下车

> get off　下车
> get on　上车
> get out　出来，取出，退出

I'll _____ here.

9. **tramp** *n.* 流浪汉

> tramp   *n.* 流浪汉
> gamin   *n.* 流浪儿
> hobo   *n.* 流浪汉，游民
> stroller   *n.* 流浪者，闲逛者

A _____ came to the door and asked for food.

10. **except** *prep.* 除……外

> except   *prep.* 除……外
> except for   除……以外，除去，要不是由于
> except that   除了……之外，只可惜
> besides   *prep.* 除……之外（包括）

I like him _____ when he's gloomy.

Ⅱ Make sentences using the under-mentioned words 单词造句

conductor — fare

_____.

change — note

_____.

passenger — get off

_____.

none — neither

_____.

tramp — except

_____.

Ⅲ Match 连线

- give and receive in return   conductor
- a piece of paper money   fare
- a person who sells tickets on a bus   change

- traveling charges　　　　　　　　　　　note
- leave a train, bus, etc.　　　　　　　　passenger
- a person with no home or job, who goes from　none
  place to place
- but not; not include　　　　　　　　　neither
- a person who is traveling in a car, bus, train,　get off
  plane, etc.
- also not　　　　　　　　　　　　　　tramp
- not any; not one　　　　　　　　　　except

Ⅳ Glossary 词汇表

conductor　n. 售票员

fare　n. 车费，车票

change　v. 兑换（钱）

note　n. 纸币

passenger　n. 乘客

none　pron. 没有任何东西

neither　adv. 也不

get off　下车

tramp　n. 流浪汉

except　prep. 除……外

Lesson 96

Knock, Knock!

敲敲门！

I New words 新单词

1. **anyone** *pron.* （用于疑问句、否定式）任何人

> anyone *pron.* （用于疑问句、否定式）任何人
> someone *pron. & n.* 某人，有人，重要人物，有名气的人
> no one 没有人，无人
> everyone *pron.* 每人，人人，各人

Has _____ seen my pen?

2. **knock** *v.* 敲，打

> knock *v.* 敲，打
> knock about 接连敲打，虐待，漂泊
> knock against 偶遇，碰见，撞上
> knock at 敲（门，窗等）
> knock cold 击倒，击昏，使目瞪口呆

_____ on the door before you enter.

3. **everything** *pron.* 一切事物

> everything *pron.* 一切事物
> anything *pron.* 任何事物；*adv.* 在任何方面，任何一点上
> something *pron.* 某事，某物
> nothing *pron.* 没有事情，一无所有

I got _____ I needed in the market.

4. **quiet** *adj.* 宁静的，安静的

> quiet *adj.* 宁静的，安静的
> quiet down 平息下来
> quiet market 不活跃的市场
> quieten *v.* 使安静，使平静
> quietish *adj.* 有点安静的

My grandmother lives a _____ life.

5. **impossible** *adj.* 不可能的

> impossible *adj.* 不可能的
> possible *adj.* 可能的
> impossibility *n.* 不可能性，办不到的事
> impossibly *adv.* 不可能地，难以置信地

It is _____ for me to pass this exam.

6. **invite** *v.* 邀请

> invite *v.* 邀请
> invitee *n.* 被邀请者，客人
> invitation *n.* 邀请，招待，请柬

We're _____ our colleagues to the party.

7. **anything** *pron.* 任何东西

> anything *pron.* 任何东西
> anything but 决不
> anything like 多少有点像
> anything of 一点儿，一点……的味儿

Is there _____ in that box?

8. **nothing** *pron.* 什么也没有

nothing　*pron.* 什么也没有
nothing but　只
nothing else but　没有别的办法
nothing if not　确实，极其，非常
nothing like　完全不像，一点儿不像

There's _____ serious.

9. **lemonade**　*n.* 柠檬水

lemonade　*n.* 柠檬水
lemon　*n.* 柠檬，柠檬色；*adj.* 柠檬的，淡黄色的
lemon drop　柠檬糖
lemon squeezer　柠檬榨汁器

She drank the _____ through a straw.

10. **joke**　*v.* 开玩笑

joke　*v.* 开玩笑
jokebook　*n.* 笑话集
joker　*n.* 爱开玩笑的人，逗趣的人
jokey　*adj.* 好开玩笑的，滑稽的
joking　*adj.* 打趣的，爱开玩笑的

You mustn't _____ with him about religious belief.

II *Make sentences using the under-mentioned words* 单词造句

anyone — knock

_____.

everything — quiet

_____.

impossible — nothing

_____.

invite — anyone

_____.

anything — joke

_____.

lemonade — drink

_____.

Ⅲ Match 连线

- with little or no noise or movement   anyone
- every object, event, fact, etc.   knock
- to strike with a blow or series of blows   everything
- whoever; any person   quiet
- to speak in fun; to play jokes   impossible
- a sweet clear drink with bubbles in it   invite
- not at all; that dose not exist   anything
- not possible   nothing
- to welcome; to speak politely to come or to do   lemonade
  something
- a thing of any kind   joke

Ⅳ Glossary 词汇表

anyone *pron.*（用于疑问句、否定式）任何人

knock *v.* 敲，打

everything *pron.* 一切事物

quiet *adj.* 宁静的，安静的

impossible *adj.* 不可能的

invite *v.* 邀请

anything *pron.* 任何东西

nothing *pron.* 什么也没有

lemonade *n.* 柠檬水

joke *v.* 开玩笑

Lesson
97

Every, no, any and some
每一、无、若干和一些

I New words 新单词

1. **asleep** *adj.* 睡觉，睡着（用作表语）

> asleep *adj.* 睡觉，睡着（用作表语）
> fall asleep 入睡，入眠，懈怠
> asleep at the switch 玩忽职守，错过机会

Is the baby still _____ ?

2. **glasses** *n.* 眼镜

> glasses *n.* 眼镜
> sunglasses *n.* 墨镜，太阳镜

She wore rimless _____ .

II Make sentences using the under-mentioned words 单词造句

asleep — glasses

_____ .

III Match 连线

- two pieces of special glass in a frame that people   asleep
  wear over their eyes to help them see
- sleeping   glasses

Ⅳ Glossary 词汇表

asleep   *adj.* 睡觉，睡着（用作表语）
glasses   *n.* 眼镜

Tommy's breakfast
汤米的早餐

I New words 新单词 ....

1. **dinning room** 饭厅

> dinning room 饭厅
> dinner 主餐，正餐
> drawing room 客厅，起居室
> living room 客厅，起居室，生活空间，居住空间

When does the _____ open?

2. **coin** *n.* 硬币

> coin *n.* 硬币
> coin machine 自动贩卖机
> coin-operated *adj.* 投入硬币即发生作用的
> coinage *n.* 铸币，造币，货币制度

I like collecting foreign _____.

3. **mouth** *n.* 嘴

> mouth *n.* 嘴
> mouth mirror 口腔镜
> mouth organ 口琴，排箫
> mouth-to-mouth *adj.* （人工呼吸）口对口的
> mouth-watering *adj.* 令人垂涎的，好像很好吃的

Open your _____ wider, please.

4. **swallow**   *v.* 吞下

> swallow   *v.* 吞下
> swallow down   吞下
> swallow up   吞没，淹没，耗尽
> swallowable   *adj.* 可吞咽的，宜于吞咽的，可靠的

Our company was _____ up by an American company last year.

5. **later**   *adv.* 后来

> later   *adv.* 后来
> later that morning   那天上午的晚些时候
> sooner or later   迟早

Some time _____ it began to rain.

6. **toilet**   *n.* 厕所，盥洗室

> toilet   *n.* 厕所，盥洗室
> toilet bowl   马桶
> toilet cover   梳妆台布
> toilet glass   梳妆镜
> toilet paper   手纸

Where is the _____?

Ⅱ *Make sentences using the under-mentioned words* 单词造句

dinning room — swallow

_____.

coin — mouth

_____.

later — toilet

_____.

III Match 连线

- bathroom; water closet
- some time after; afterwards
- make food or drink move down your throat from your mouth
- a room where people eat
- a round piece of money made of metal
- the part of your face below your nose that you use for eating and speaking

dinning room

coin

mouth

swallow

later

toilet

IV Glossary 词汇表

dinning room 饭厅
coin *n.* 硬币
mouth *n.* 嘴
swallow *v.* 吞下
later *adv.* 后来
toilet *n.* 厕所，盥洗室

A true story

一个真实的故事

I New words 新单词

1. **story** *n.* 故事

> story *n.* 故事
> make up a story 编造一个故事
> as the story goes 正像人们传说的
> be another story 又是一会事
> the same old story 还是那一套

The film was adapted from a true _____.

2. **happen** *v.* 发生

> happen *v.* 发生
> it happens to sb. 发生在……身上
> happen along 偶然出现，碰巧来到
> happen on/upon 偶然遇到，偶然发现
> happen to 发生于，临到

How did the accident _____?

3. **thief** *n.* （复数 thieves）贼

> thief *n.* （复数 thieves）贼
> thieve *v.* 作贼，窃取
> thievery *n.* 偷窃，窃物，赃物

The _____ was sent to prison.

4. **enter** *v.* 进入

> enter *v.* 进入
>
> enter for （为……）报名参加
>
> enter in 进入
>
> enter into 进入，参加，开始从事
>
> enterable *adj.* 可进入的

The bullet _____ his heart.

5. **dark** *adj.* 黑暗的

> dark *adj.* 黑暗的
>
> dark-adapted *adj.* （眼睛）暗适应的
>
> Dark Ages 黑暗时代（欧洲中世纪的早期）
>
> darken *v.* 变黑，使处于黑暗中

It was a _____ , moonless night.

6. **torch** *n.* 手电筒

> torch *n.* 手电筒
>
> torchier *n.* 间接照明落地灯
>
> torchlight *n.* 火炬之光
>
> torch race 火炬接力赛

He used a _____ to see into the dark cupboard.

7. **voice** *n.* （说话的）声音

> voice *n.* （说话的）声音
>
> voice box 喉头
>
> voice-over *adj.* 话外音的，旁白的
>
> sound *n.* 声音，声调，响声
>
> noise *n.* 声音，噪音

I've lost my _____ .

8. **parrot**   *n.* 鹦鹉

> parrot   *n.* 鹦鹉
>
> as a parrot   鹦鹉学舌似地重复
>
> parrotry   *n.* 重复学话

Sometimes children repeat their lessons as a _____.

II *Make sentences using the under-mentioned words* 单词造句

story — happen

_____ .

thief — enter

_____ .

dark — torch

_____ .

voice — parrot

_____ .

III Match 连线

- species of hook-billed tropical birds with bright-colored feathers, some of which can be trained to imitate human speech   story
- sound   happen
- small hand-held electric lamp   thief
- with little or without any light   enter
- account of factual or fictitious events; tale   dark
- occur; take place   torch
- one who steals   voice
- account of past events, incidents, etc.   parrot

Ⅳ Glossary 词汇表

story　*n.* 故事

happen　*v.* 发生

thief　*n.* （复数 thieves）贼

enter　*v.* 进入

dark　*adj.* 黑暗的

torch　*n.* 手电筒

voice　*n.* （说话的）声音

parrot　*n.* 鹦鹉

Lesson 100

The man in a hat
戴帽子的男士

I New words 新单词

1. **customer** *n.* 顾客

> customer   *n.* 顾客
> buyer   *n.* 买主，顾客，采购员
> client   *n.* 委托人，顾客，客户

The store has a lot of regular _____.

2. **forget** *v.* 忘记

> forget   *v.* 忘记
> forget about it   不必在意，休想，不可能
> forget-me-not   *n.* 勿忘我
> forget oneself   先人后己，忘我，心不在焉
> forget to do sth.   忘记去做某事
> forget doing sth.   忘记做了某事

I'll never _____ meeting her for the first time.

3. **manager** *n.* 经理

> manager   *n.* 经理
> manageress   *n.* 女经理，女管理人，女助理
> managerial   *adj.* 经理的，管理的

He is an excellent _____.

4. **serve** *v.* 照应，服务，接待

> serve *v.* 照应，服务，接待
> serve for 充当，用做
> server *n.* 侍者，上菜者

What time is breakfast _____ in this hotel?

5. **counter** *n.* 柜台

> counter *n.* 柜台
> counter card 柜台上之广告牌

I bought the necklace at the jewelry _____.

6. **recognize** *v.* 认出

> recognize *v.* 认出
> recognition *n.* 认可，确认，承认，赏识
> recognitory *adj.* 承认的，认识的

Can you _____ this tune?

Ⅱ *Make sentences using the under-mentioned words* 单词造句

customer — serve

_____.

forget — counter

_____.

manager — recognize

_____.

Ⅲ *Match* 连线

· ·

- to identify from previous experiences; to realize   customer
- a flat surface on which goods are transacted   forget
- to be a servant to; to attend   manager

- a person who pays for goods or services in a shop etc.　serve
- not remember sth.　counter
- person in charge of a business　recognize

Ⅳ Glossary 词汇表

customer　*n.* 顾客

forget　*v.* 忘记

manager　*n.* 经理

serve　*v.* 照应，服务，接待

counter　*n.* 柜台

recognize　*v.* 认出

Lesson 101

Who (whom), which and that 关系代词

I New words 新单词

1. **road** *n.* 路

> road *n.* 路
> road junction 三岔路
> road map 街道地图
> road metal 铺路用的碎石

This is a _____ to success.

II Make sentences using the under-mentioned words 单词造句

road — wide

_____.

III Match 连线

- open way for persons, vehicle   road

IV Glossary 词汇表

road *n.* 路

Lesson 102

A trip to Australia
澳大利亚之行

1. **during** *prep.* 在……期间

   Don't speak _____ the meal.

2. **trip** *n.* 旅行

trip *n.* 旅行
business trip 商务旅行，出差
travel *v.* 旅行，旅游
journey *n.* 旅途，旅行

   He has gone on a business _____.

3. **travel** *v.* 旅行

travel *v.* 旅行
travel agency 旅行社
travel service 旅行社
travel agent 旅行代理人

   He said that if he had a lot of money he would _____ around the world.

4. **offer** *v.* 提供

offer *v.* 提供
offer to treat 提议自己出钱请人吃饭，喝酒或

做其他的娱乐

offering   *n.* 提供，贡献，赠品，祭品

We _____ some coffee to the guests.

5. **job**   *n.* 工作

> job   *n.* 工作
> job center   职业介绍中心
> job class   工作分类，职位分类
> job consciousness   职业道德，职业意识
> job description   工作说明
> work   *n. & v.* 工作

The teacher's _____ is very important.

6. **guess**   *v.* 猜

> guess   *v.* 猜
> guessable   *adj.* 可猜测的，可推测的
> guessing   *adv.* 凭猜测
> guesswork   *n.* 猜测，猜测的结果

I _____ it will rain tomorrow.

7. **grow** (grew/grown)   *v.* 长，让……生长

> grow (grew/grown)   *v.* 长，让……生长
> grow apart   （植物）朝不同的方向生长
> grow away from   离开……生长，同……疏远起来
> grow downwards   （植物等）向下生长，缩小，减少
> grow into   成长（或发展）为……，长得适合
>   于……
> grow up   长成，成熟，发展

The trees have _____ rapidly.

8. **beard**　*n.*（下巴上的）胡子，络腮胡子

> beard　*n.*（下巴上的）胡子，络腮胡子
> bearded　*adj.* 有须子的，有芒的
> beardless　*adj.* 无胡子的，无芒的

The man with a _____ looks familiar.

Ⅱ Make sentences using the under-mentioned words 单词造句

during — trip

_____.

travel — guess

_____.

offer — job

_____.

grow — beard

_____.

Ⅲ Match 连线

- to hold out for acceptance or refusal　　　during
- work　　　trip
- throughout the course of　　　travel
- journey　　　offer
- hair which grows on a man's chin and cheeks　　　job
- the development of living plants or animals　　　guess
- give an answer based on supposition　　　grow（grew/grown）
- to go from one place to another, esp. to a distant place　　　beard

IV *Glossary* 词汇表

during   *prep.* 在……期间

trip   *n.* 旅行

travel   *v.* 旅行

offer   *v.* 提供

job   *n.* 工作

guess   *v.* 猜

grow（grew/grown）   *v.* 长，让……生长

beard   *n.*（下巴上的）胡子，络腮胡子

Lesson 103

(who) / (whom), (which) and (that)   关系代词

I New words 新单词

1. **kitten**   *n.* 小猫

> kitten   *n.* 小猫
> kittenish   *adj.* 小猫似的，耍闹的
> cat   *n.* 猫，猫科动物

Bob is playing with the _____.

II Make sentences using the under-mentioned words 单词造句

kitten — like

_____.

III Match 连线

• young cat   kitten

IV Glossary 词汇表

◼ kitten   *n.* 小猫

Tea for two
两个人一起喝茶

Ⅰ New words 新单词

1. **water** *v.* 浇水

> water *v.* 浇水
>
> water bag 水袋
>
> water baler 水上芭蕾舞
>
> water bed 水床，充水床垫

Tim is _____ his lovely little dog.

2. **terribly** *adv.* 非常

> terribly *adv.* 非常
>
> terrible *adj.* 可怕的，糟糕的
>
> very *adv.* 非常，极其

I'm _____ sorry.

3. **dry** *adj.* 干燥的，干的

> dry *adj.* 干燥的，干的
>
> dry battery 干电池
>
> dry-bones *n.* 骨瘦如柴之人
>
> dry-clean *v.* 干洗
>
> dry cleaner 干洗商，干洗店

The paint is not yet _____.

4. **nuisance**   *n.* 讨厌的东西或人

> nuisance   *n.* 讨厌的东西或人
> What a nuisance! 真讨厌!
> bother   *n.* & *v.* 讨厌的人或事物, 打扰, 麻烦
> annoyance   讨厌的人或东西

Don't make a _____ of yourself.

5. **mean**（meant/meant）   *v.* 意味着, 意思是

> mean（meant/meant）   *v.* 意味着, 意思是
> It means that...   那就意味着……
> What does... mean?   意思是什么?

The green light _____ "Go on".

6. **surprise**   *n.* 惊奇, 意外的事

> surprise   *n.* 惊奇, 意外的事
> surprise party   惊喜聚会
> surprisedly   *adj.* 惊奇地, 诧异地
> surprising   *adv.* 令人惊奇地, 出乎意外地
> to one's surprise   使……感到吃惊（意外）

To my _____ , he refused to go with us.

Ⅱ *Make sentences using the under-mentioned words* 单词造句

water — dry

_____.

terribly — nuisance

_____.

mean — surprise

_____.

III Match 连线

- a feeling of wonder or amazement   water
- have as a meaning   terribly
- a person or thing that causes you trouble dry
- the liquid in rivers, lakes and seas that nuisance
  people and animals drink
- very   mean (meant/meant)
- not wet; with no liquid in it or on it   surprise

IV Glossary 词汇表

water   *v.* 浇水
terribly   *adv.* 非常
dry   *adj.* 干燥的，干的
nuisance   *n.* 讨厌的东西或人
mean (meant/meant)   *v.* 意味着，意思是
surprise   *n.* 惊奇，意外的事

Lesson 105

Have to and do not need to
不得不和不必要

I New words 新单词

1. **immediately** *adv.* 立即地

> immediately *adv.* 立即地
> immediate *adj.* 快速地，直接地，即刻地
> at once 立刻

I came _____ I heard the news.

II Make sentences using the under-mentioned words 单词造句

immediately — come

_____.

III Match 连线

- at once   immediately

IV Glossary 词汇表

■ immediately *adv.* 立即地

Lesson 106

A famous actress
著名的女演员

1. **famous** *adj.* 著名的

> famous *adj.* 著名的
> be famous for 以……而出名
> be famous as 作为……而出名
> famously *adv.* 著名地，出名地，非常

He is _____ as a writer.

2. **actress** *n.* 女演员

> actress *n.* 女演员
> actor *n.* 男演员
> act *n. v.* 表演，行为

Her aunt is a very popular _____.

3. **at least** 至少

> at least 至少
> least *adj.* 最小的，最少的
> leastways *adv.* 至少，无论如何
> at lowest 至少

This antique vase is worth _____ 20,000.

4. **actor**   *n.* 男演员

> actor   *n.* 男演员
> actorish   *adj.* 男演员的，参与的，行动的

He is considered the best _____ in London.

5. **read**（read/read）   *v.* 通过阅读得知

> read（read/read）   *v.* 通过阅读得知
> read about   阅读而知
> read back   重读一遍
> read for   攻读
> read on   念下去

We _____ about the storm in the paper today.

Ⅱ *Make sentences using the under-mentioned words* 单词造句

famous — actress

_____.

at least — three

_____.

actor — read

_____.

Ⅲ Match 连线

- at lowest   famous
- to be well-known or popular   actress
- a female theatrical performance   at least
- to undersatand or comprehend meaning of   actor
- a male theatrical performance   read（read/read）

IV Glossary 词汇表

famous *adj.* 著名的
actress *n.* 女演员
at least 至少
actor *n.* 男演员
read (read/read) *v.* 通过阅读得知

Lesson
107
Seventy miles an hour
时速 70 英里

Ⅰ New words 新单词 ·······································

1. wave *v.* 招手

> wave *v.* 招手
> wave sb. goodbye 向某人挥手告别
> wave to/at sb. 朝某人挥手

She _____ me goodbye.

2. track *n.* 跑道

> track *n.* 跑道
> track and field 田径运动
> track down 追捕到，搜寻到
> track man 田径运动员

He runs around the _____ every morning.

3. mile *n.* 英里

> mile *n.* 英里
> mileage *n.* 英里里程，英里数
> milemeter *n.* 汽车记程计

He drives 10 _____ each day to and from his work.

4. overtake（overtook/overtaken） *v.* 从后面超越，超车

overtake（overtook/overtaken） v. 从后面超越，
超车
overtaking n. 超车

The car _____ the truck.

5. **speed limit** 限速

speed limit 限速
speed trap 汽车超速监视区
speed up 加快速度

What's the _____ here?

6. **dream** v. 做梦，思想不集中

dream v. 做梦，思想不集中
dream about 做梦，梦到
dream away/out 不住地出神，梦幻般度过
dream of 梦见，梦到

Do you often _____ at night?

7. **sign** n. 标记，牌子

sign n. 标记，牌子
sign away 签字给予或放弃
sign in 使签到，使报道

The _____ by the road said "No Parking".

8. **driving licence** 驾驶执照

driving licence 驾驶执照
driving wheel 驱动轮，主动轮

His _____ had been endorsed.

9. **charge** v. 罚款

charge　v. 罚款

charge account　赊欠户，赊购制

charge against　控告

charge for　为……收费

He was _____ for speeding.

10. **darling**　n. 亲爱的（用作表示称呼）

darling　n. 亲爱的（用作表示称呼）

dear　adj. 亲爱的，可爱的，贵重的

beloved　n. 所爱的人，亲爱的教友们；adj. 所钟爱的，被热爱的

_____ , go now, or you will be late.

II Make sentences using the under-mentioned words 单词造句

wave — darling

_____.

track — overtake

_____.

mile — speed limit

_____.

dream — sign

_____.

driving licence — charge

_____.

III Match 连线

- dear
- record as a debt

wave

track

- move one's hand from side to side in the air to say goodbye or to make a sign to sb   mile
- a piece of paper that shows you that you are allowed to drive a car   overtake (overtook/overtaken)
- something that signifies the presence of an object, condition, or quality   speed limit
- course made for a certain purpose as for racing   dream
- uint for measuring distance   sign
- catch up with and pass   driving licence
- series of events pictured in one's mind while sleep   charge
- the fastest that you are allowed to travel on a road   darling

Ⅳ Glossary 词汇表

wave *v.* 招手

track *n.* 跑道

mile *n.* 英里

overtake (overtook/overtaken) *v.* 从后面超越，超车

speed limit 限速

dream *v.* 做梦，思想不集中

sign *n.* 标记，牌子

driving licence 驾驶执照

charge *v.* 罚款

darling *n.* 亲爱的（用作表示称呼）

Don't be so sure!
别那么肯定！

I New words 新单词

1. **Egypt** *n.* 埃及

> Egypt *n.* 埃及
> Egyptian *adj. &n.* 埃及人的，埃及语的；埃及人

_____ is an ancient country.

2. **abroad** *adv.* 国外

> abroad *adv.* 国外
> overseas *adv. & adj.* 在国外，在海外；海外的，
> 国外的

Her son is still studying _____.

3. **worry** *v.* 担忧

> worry *v.* 担忧
> worry too much 顾虑重重
> worry about... 担心……

My parents _____ if I come home late.

II Make sentences using the under-mentioned words 单词造句

Egypt — abroad

_____.

worry — about

_____.

III Match 连线

- to be in or go to foreign places   Egypt
- feeling uneasy or troubled   abroad
- a country in Northeastern Africa whose capital is Cairo   worry

IV Glossary 词汇表

Egypt   *n.* 埃及
abroad   *adv.* 国外
worry   *v.* 担忧

Sensational news!
爆炸性新闻！

1. **reporter**   *n.* 记者

> reporter   *n.* 记者
> report   *n. & v.* 报道，报告
> pressman   *n.* 新闻记者，印刷工

He becomes a _____ for China Daily.

2. **sensational**   *adj.* 爆炸性的，耸人听闻的

> sensational   *adj.* 爆炸性的，耸人听闻的
> sensation   *n.* 轰动一时的事件或人物

The discovery was _____.

3. **mink coat**   貂皮大衣

> mink coat   貂皮大衣
> mink   *n.* 貂，貂皮，时髦女郎

She had the only full-length _____ in our town.

reporter —— sensational

_____.

mink coat — expensive

_____.

III Match 连线

- very exciting or interesting   reporter
- a kind of coat made of the fur of the mink   sensational
- person who report news for newspaper or   mink coat
  broadcasting

IV Glossary 词汇表

reporter   *n.* 记者
sensational   *adj.* 爆炸性的，耸人听闻的
mink coat   貂皮大衣

Lesson 110

The latest report
最新消息

1. **future** *n.* 未来的

> future   *n.* 未来的
> future life   来世
> futureless   *adj.* 无前途的，无希望的

He met his _____ wife at a dance.

2. **get married** 结婚

> get married   结婚
> marry sb. /be married to sb.   和……结婚
> divorce   离婚

You are too young to _____ .

3. **hotel** *n.* 饭店

> hotel   *n.* 饭店
> hotelier   *n.* 旅馆老板，旅馆经理
> inn   *n.* 小旅馆，小饭店
> lodging   *n.* 寄宿处，住处，寓所
> motel   *n.* 汽车旅馆
> restaurant   *n.* 餐馆，餐厅，饭店

We stayed at a resort _____ during the holidays.

4. **latest** *adj.* 最新的

> latest   *adj.* 最新的
> latest price-list   最新价目表
> at latest   最晚，至迟

She dressed in the _____ Paris fashion.

5. **introduce** *v.* 介绍

> introduce   *v.* 介绍
> introduce sb. to sb.   介绍相识
> introduce into   插入

May I _____ myself?

II Make sentences using the under-mentioned words 单词造句

future — get married

_____.

hotel — latest

_____.

introduce — to

_____.

III Match 连线

- make people known to another   future
- a public house that provides beds and meals for   get
- travelers   married
- newest   hotel
- the time that will come   latest
- take as a husband or wife   introduce

IV *Glossary* 词汇表

future　*n.* 未来的
get married　结婚
hotel　*n.* 饭店
latest　*adj.* 最新的
introduce　*v.* 介绍

A pleasant dream
美好的梦

I New words 新单词

1. **football** *n.* 足球

> football   *n.* 足球
> footballer   *n.* 足球运动员，橄榄球运动员
> soccer   ＜美＞足球
> do the football pool   做足球赌注
> football fan   足球迷

He is a crazy _____ fan.

2. **pool** *n.* 赌注

> pool   *n.* 赌注
> do the football pool   做足球赌注
> ante   *n.* 赌注，所需的款项，价格
> stake   *n.* 赌注，赌本
> wager   *n.* & *v.* 打赌，赌博，赌注

He does the football _____ every week.

3. **win** (won/won)   *v.* 赢

> win (won/won)   *v.* 赢
> win a bid   中标
> win a seat   在国会选举中当选

He felt very excited to have _____ the gold medal.

4. **world**   *n.* 世界

> world   *n.* 世界
> in the world   在世界上
> see the world   看世界
> travel round the world   周游世界

The blind people live in a dark _____.

5. **poor**   *adj.* 贫穷的

> poor   *adj.* 贫穷的
> poor as a church   一贫如洗
> poor box   慈善箱，捐款箱
> poor crop   欠收
> poor farm   救济农场

My family used to be _____.

6. **depend**   *v.* 依靠（on）

> depend   *v.* 依靠（on）
> depend on/upon   依靠，依赖，取决于，从属于
> dependable   *adj.* 可靠的，可信任的
> dependability   *n.* 可靠性，可信任

I knew he wasn't to be _____ on.

Ⅱ *Make sentences using the under-mentioned words* 单词造句

football — win

_____.

pool — depend

_____.

world — poor

_____.

Ⅲ Match 连线

- rely, as for support; place trust   football
- having little money or means   pool
- the earth with all its countries and people   win（won/won）
- a game for two teams of eleven players   world
  who try to kick a ball into a goal
- stake in games   poor
- get a victory; beat all the others in a contest   depend

Ⅳ Glossary 词汇表

football   *n.* 足球

pool   *n.* 赌注

win（won/won）   *v.* 赢

world   *n.* 世界

poor   *adj.* 贫穷的

depend   *v.* 依靠（on）

Lesson 112

Is that you, John?
是你吗，约翰？

I　New words　新单词

1. **extra**　*adj.*　额外的

> extra　*adj.*　额外的
> extra allowance　额外津贴
> extra-atmospheric　*adj.*　大气层外的

Could you get an _____ bottle of milk?

2. **overseas**　*adj.*　海外的，国外的

> overseas　*adj.*　海外的，国外的
> overseas agent　国外代理人
> overseas investment　海外投资
> overseas money order　国外汇票

They want to open up the _____ market.

3. **engineering**　*n.*　工程

> engineering　*n.*　工程
> engineer　*n.*　工程师，设计者，发明者
> engineering science　工程学
> engineering workstation　工程工作站

He is studying _____ at college.

4. **company**　*n.*　公司

> company   *n.* 公司
> firm   *n. & adj.* 公司，坚固的，牢固的
> association   *n.* 公司，协会
> enterprise   *n.* 企业，公司

He is working in a shipping _____.

5. **line**   *n.* 线路

> line   *n.* 线路
> line code   线路代码
> line drawing   线条画，素描
> line extender   线路延长器
> line is busy   线路忙，讲话中

A new bus _____ runs straight to the airport.

Ⅱ Make sentences using the under-mentioned words 单词造句

extra — work

_____.

overseas — company

_____.

engineering — line

_____.

Ⅲ Match 连线

- a very long wire for telephones or electricity   extra
- a group of people who work together to make   work
  or sell things
- planning and making things like machines,   overseas
  roads or bridges

- more than what is usual　　　　　　　　　engineering
- job　　　　　　　　　　　　　　　　　　company
- in, to or from another country across the sea　line

Ⅳ Glossary 词汇表

extra　*adj.* 额外的

overseas　*adj.* 海外的，国外的

engineering　*n.* 工程

company　*n.* 公司

line　*n.* 线路

Lesson 113

Sally's first train ride
萨莉第一次乘火车旅行

I New words 新单词

1. **excited** *adj.* 兴奋的

> excited   *adj.* 兴奋的
> exciting   *adj.* 令人兴奋的
> excited insects   惊蛰
> excitedly   *adv.* 兴奋地，激动地

The _____ old lady soon calmed down.

2. **get on** 登上

> get on   登上
> get away   （汽车）起步，走开，离开
> get back   返回，取回，恢复
> get off   下来，下（马，自行车，火车，飞机等）

Please wait your turn to _____ the bus.

3. **middle-aged** *adj.* 中年的

> middle-aged   *adj.* 中年的
> middle   *adj.* 中部的，中间的，中庸的
> middle age   中年
> middler agern 中年人

There comes a _____ man.

4. **opposite**   *prep.* 在……对面

> opposite   *prep.* 在……对面
> opposite number   对应的人或物
> opposite sex   异性
> oppositely   *adv.* 相对地
> opposition   *n.* 反对，反抗，敌对

The post office is _____ the bank.

5. **curiously**   *adv.* 好奇地

> curiously   *adv.* 好奇地
> curious   *adj.* 好奇的，求知的，古怪的
> curiousness   *n.* 好奇，好学
> curiosity   *n.* 好奇心，求知欲

She _____ opened the letter addressed to her husband.

6. **funny**   *adj.* 可笑的，滑稽的

> funny   *adj.* 可笑的，滑稽的
> funny bone   幽默感
> funny business   胡闹，欺骗，不端行为
> funnyman   *n.* 小丑，滑稽演员，幽默家

I heard such a _____ joke last night.

7. **powder**   *n.* 香粉

> powder   *n.* 香粉
> powder box   化妆盒
> powder puff   粉扑，粉球
> powder room   化妆室
> powdered   *adj.* 涂了粉的，弄成粉的

There's too much _____ on your nose.

8. **compact** *n.* 带镜的化妆盒

> compact *n.* 带镜的化妆盒
> dressing case 梳妆盒，梳妆箱
> powder box 化妆盒

She has an exquisite _____.

9. **kindly** *adv.* 和蔼地

> kindly *adv.* 和蔼地
> kind *adj.* 和蔼的，好的，仁慈的，体贴的
> kindhearted *adj.* 好心的，仁慈的
> kindles *adj.* 冷酷的，无人性的

He treats the children _____.

10. **ugly** *adj.* 丑陋的

> ugly *adj.* 丑陋的
> ugly customer 讨厌而令人生畏的人，难对付的
>   家伙，危险分子
> ugly duck 丑小鸭

He has put an _____ stone head over the gate.

11. **amused** *adj.* 有趣的

> amused *adj.* 有趣的
> amusedly *adv.* 愉快地，好玩地，开心地
> amusement *n.* 趣味，娱乐，消遣
> amusement park 公共露天游乐场

She wore on her face an _____ look.

12. **smile** *v.* 微笑

> smile *v.* 微笑
> smiling *adj.* 微笑的，欢笑的

> laugh　*v.* 发笑，笑出
> grin　露齿而笑，咧嘴而笑

The bridegroom was _____ broadly.

13. **embarrassed**　*adj.* 尴尬的，窘迫的

> embarrassed　*adj.* 尴尬的，窘迫的
> embarrass　*v.* 局促不安，使尴尬
> embarrassment　*n.* 尴尬
> embarrassedly　*adv.* 尴尬地，难堪地
> embarrassing　*adj.* 使人尴尬的，使人难堪的

I was very _____ by his comments.

Ⅱ Make sentences using the under-mentioned words 单词造句

excited — smile

_____.

get on — opposite

_____.

curiously — funny

_____.

middle — aged — kindly

_____.

powder — compact

_____.

ugly — embarrassed

_____.

amused — story

_____.

III Match 连线

- set against；totally different
- between the ages of about 40 to 60
- not beautiful to look at
- climb onto a bus, train or bike
- a powder box that with a mirror on it
- substance crushed or ground to fine dry particles, as for cosmetic oe medical purpose
- eager to know something
- causing amusement
- feel shy or worried about what other people think of you
- not calm, for example because you are happy about something that is going to happen
- in a kind and friendly way
- interesting
- laugh

excited
get on
middle-aged
opposite
curiously
funny

powder
compact
kindly

ugly

amused
smile
embarrassed

IV Glossary 词汇表

excited *adj.* 兴奋的
get on 登上
middle-aged *adj.* 中年的
opposite *prep.* 在……对面
curiously *adv.* 好奇地
funny *adj.* 可笑的，滑稽的
powder *n.* 香粉
compact *n.* 带镜的化妆盒
kindly *adv.* 和蔼地
ugly *adj.* 丑陋的

amused　*adj.* 有趣的

smile　*v.* 微笑

embarrassed　*adj.* 尴尬的，窘迫的

Lesson 114

Someone invited Sally to a party.
有人邀请萨莉出席一个聚会。
Sally was invited to a party.
萨莉应邀出席一个聚会。

I New words 新单词

1. **worried** *adj.* 担心，担忧

> worried *adj.* 担心，担忧
> worry *n. & v.* 担心，发愁
> worrier *n.* 担心的人，发愁的人
> worriless *adj.* 无忧无虑的，毫不担心的
> worry about 担心

People are becoming increasingly _____ about pollution.

2. **regularly** *adv.* 经常地，定期的

> regularly *adv.* 经常地，定期的
> regular *adj.* 定期的，正常的，固定的
> regularity *n.* 经常，定期，规则性，一致
> regularize *v.* 使规律化，使条理化

We meet _____ to discuss business.

II Make sentences using the under-mentioned words 单词造句

worried — regularly

_____.

III Match 连线

- usually; things happens again and again with the same amount of time in between

worried

- unhappy because you think that sth bad will happen or has happened

regularly

IV Glossary 词汇表

worried　　*adj.* 担心的，担忧的
regularly　*adv.* 经常地，定期的

A walk through the woods
林中散步

I New words 新单词

1. **surround** *v.* 包围

> surround *v.* 包围
> surrounding *adj.* 周围的，环绕的；*n.* 围绕物，
>   环境
> surroundings *n.* 周围的事物（环境），环境

That old professor loved do _____ himself with young people.

2. **wood** *n.* 树林

> wood *n.* 树林
> wood block　木刻的，木版的
> wood carving　木雕，木雕品
> wood chopper　樵夫，伐木者
> wood coal　木炭，褐煤

He was lost in the _____.

3. **beauty spot** 风景点

> beauty spot　风景点
> landscape　风景
> scenery *n.* 景色，风景

The Great Wall is a world-famous _____.

4. **hundred**　*n.* 百

> hundred　*n.* 百
>
> hundreds of　好几百，许许多多
>
> hundreds of thousands of　几十万，无数

The child can count from one to a _____.

5. **city**　*n.* 城市

> city　*n.* 城市
>
> city-bred　*adj.* 生长在（大）城市的
>
> city center　（城镇的）中心区，商业区
>
> city council　市政会，市议会

They live in New York _____.

6. **through**　*prep.* 穿过

> through　*prep.* 穿过
>
> through the medium of　通过，以……为媒介
>
> through-hole　穿孔
>
> through and through　完全，彻底

The thief got in _____ the window.

7. **visitor**　*n.* 参观者，游客，来访者

> visitor　*n.* 参观者，游客，来访者
>
> visit　*v.* 参观，旅游
>
> traveler　*n.* 旅行者，旅客

There are many _____ to the White House every year.

8. **tidy**　*adj.* 整齐的

> tidy　*adj.* 整齐的
>
> tidy away　收拾起来
>
> tidy-up　*n.* 整理，收拾

Her room is always clean and _____.

9. **litter** *n.* 杂乱的东西

litter *n.* 杂乱的东西

litter-lout *n.* 在公共场所乱仍废物的人

litter up 乱丢废物，使混乱

junk *n.* 废品，破烂货

rubbish *n.* 垃圾

There are piles of _____ on the streets after a parade.

10. **litter basket** 废物筐

litter basket 废物筐

garbage can 垃圾桶

garbage truck 垃圾车

Please throw all waste paper into the _____.

11. **place** *v.* 放

place *v.* 放

place a loan 发放贷款

place money 投放资金

He _____ the record back to the shelf.

12. **throw**（threw/thrown） *v.* 扔，抛

throw（threw/thrown） *v.* 扔，抛

throw about 乱丢，乱花钱

throw at 向……扔去

throw away 扔掉，抛弃

throw back 扔回

He _____ the book on the table.

13. **rubbish** *n.* 垃圾

rubbish   *n.* 垃圾
junk   *n.* 垃圾，废品
garbage   *n.* 垃圾

Our job is to clear away the _____ .

14. **count**   *v.* 数，点

count   *v.* 数，点
count in one's head   心算
count on   指望
count out   点清，被判失败
count up   把……加起来

They are _____ the books they collected.

15. **cover**   *v.* 覆盖

cover   *v.* 覆盖
cover charge   小费，服务费
cover over   遮没
cover up   掩盖，隐藏，包裹
be covered with...   覆盖着……

She _____ the table with a cloth.

16. **piece**   *n.* 碎片

piece   *n.* 碎片
piece goods   布匹，匹头
pieceable   *adj.* 可接合的，可修补的
a piece of   一块，一片

She took a _____ of cake.

17. **tyre**   *n.* 轮胎

tyre   *n.* 轮胎
tread   *n.* 轮胎面，车胎胎面花纹

I have to get my front _____ blown up.

18. **rusty** *adj.* 生锈的

> rusty *adj.* 生锈的
> rust *n. & v. & adj.* 锈；生锈；铁锈色的
> rust-resistant *adj.* 抗锈的，不锈的

The machine is getting _____.

19. **among** *prep.* 在……之间

> among *prep.* 在……之间
> amid *prep.* 在其中，在正当中
> between *prep.* 在……（两者）之间

She has always been popular _____ his classmates.

20. **prosecute** *v.* 依法处置

> prosecute *v.* 依法处置
> prosecution *n.* 起诉，告发，检举
> prosecutor *n.* 起诉人，原告

They _____ him for shoplifting.

Ⅱ *Make sentences using the under-mentioned words* 单词造句

surround — wood

_____.

beauty spot — city

_____.

hundred — visitor

_____.

through — litter

_____.

tidy — place

_____.

litter basket — rubbish

_____.

throw — piece

_____.

tyre — among

_____.

rusty — iron

_____.

Ⅲ Match 连线

- a number 100; ten times ten
- places with beautiful scenery
- be or go all around something
- a big group of trees
- with everything in the right place
- traveler; people who go to see another people or place for a short time
- a big and important town
- from one side or end of something to the other side or end
- move your arm quickly to send something through the air
- put something somewhere
- pieces of paper and other things that people leave on the ground
- basket used for putting litter in

- a part of something
- be all over something

surround
wood
beauty spot
hundred
city
through

visitor
tidy

litter

litter basket
place

throw (threw/
thrown)
rubbish
count

- things that you do not want any more   cover
- look at people or things to see how many there are   piece
- to take legal act against   tyre
- between one another; surrounded by   rusty
- a rubber covering around the rim of the wheel to absorb shocks   among
- covered with rust   prosecute

IV Glossary 词汇表

surround   *v.* 包围
wood   *n.* 树林
beauty spot   风景点
hundred   *n.* 百
city   *n.* 城市
through   *prep.* 穿过
visitor   *n.* 参观者，游客，来访者
tidy   *adj.* 整齐的
litter   *n.* 杂乱的东西
litter basket   废物筐
place   *v.* 放
throw (threw/thrown)   *v.* 扔，抛
rubbish   *n.* 垃圾
count   *v.* 数，点
cover   *v.* 覆盖
piece   *n.* 碎片
tyre   *n.* 轮胎
rusty   *adj.* 生锈的
among   *prep.* 在……之间
prosecute   *v.* 依法处置